CARNIVAL
of the
HUNTED

FABER has published children's books since 1929. T. S. Eliot's *Old Possum's Book of Practical Cats* and Ted Hughes' *The Iron Man* were among the first. Our catalogue at the time said that 'it is by reading such books that children learn the difference between the shoddy and the genuine'. We still believe in the power of reading to transform children's lives. All our books are chosen with the express intention of growing a love of reading, a thirst for knowledge and to cultivate empathy. We pride ourselves on responsible editing. Last but not least, we believe in kind and inclusive books in which all children feel represented and important.

Kieran Larwood was born in Kenya. He moved to the UK when he was two and lived in various places before settling on the Isle of Wight, where he can still be found: exploring rockpools, climbing trees and writing. He taught Reception class in a primary school for fifteen years before becoming a full-time author. Kieran's books have won several awards, including the Blue Peter Best Story and the Prix Sorcières. He is inspired by a life-long love of fantasy stories, which all began when – as a young boy – he picked up a copy of *The Hobbit* and saw the map inside. It just goes to show – you never know where opening a book will lead . . .

Sam Usher is a multi-award-winning illustrator. His books include the Seasons series, *The Birthday Duck, The Most-Loved Bear* and *The Umbrella Mouse.* Also a talented pianist, when he's not scribbling you'll find him perfecting a fiendishly difficult Chopin piece.

THE CARNIVAL SERIES

Carnival of the Lost

Carnival of the Hunted

THE FIVE REALMS SERIES

The Legend of Podkin One-Ear

The Gift of Dark Hollow

The Beasts of Grimheart

Uki and the Outcasts

Uki and the Swamp Spirit

Uki and the Ghostburrow

KIERAN LARWOOD

Illustrated by Sam Usher

faber

First published in 2022
by Faber & Faber Limited
Bloomsbury House,
74–77 Great Russell Street,
London WC1B 3DA
faberchildrens.co.uk

Typeset in Times New Roman by MRules
Printed by CPI Group (UK) Ltd,
Croydon CR0 4YY

A CIP record for this book is available from the British Library

ISBN 978–0–571–36452–7

2 4 6 8 10 9 7 5 3 1

For Jenny

PROLOGUE

LONDON, SEPTEMBER 1861

There is a full moon tonight. A hunter's moon. It hangs high in the sky, setting the great house's grounds alight with silver. The wide, gravel-lined driveway, the immaculate lawns. Everything sparkles, as if it were midday in some strange, colourless new world.

At the edge of the manor grounds are the woods. The hunters' woods.

Here the moon paints shadows. Black like spilled ink, thick with hidden secrets. The woods are filled with rustles and squeaks, noises of creatures hiding, burrowing and roosting. Mostly small, furry or feathered ones, but tonight there is something bigger. Much bigger.

You can hear it panting. Its mewls echo between the trees and black-lined bushes. Twigs snap under its feet as it stumbles and crashes over roots. Whispered curses slip from its lips as it is ripped and tripped by thorns and brambles.

Another sound: the soft creak of leather and the yawning stretch of a crossbow string. A click as the catch locks and a slither of wood as the bolt is fitted.

One of the moon's shadows moves, peeling itself away from a tree trunk to stand for a moment inside a patch of silver light.

Not a shadow, then: a man. A fox-man. Dressed head to foot in hunting leather – some kind of glinting smoked-glass goggles hiding his face – and two pointed fox ears jutting from his head.

A heartbeat, and then another figure joins him, raising an arm to point in the direction of the blundering, sobbing sounds. This one has the ears of a wolf, shaggy grey fur framing his goggles, covering his mouth.

This is their wood, their moon. They are the hunters, and they have found their prey.

The first figure raises his crossbow, tilting his head to pinpoint the exact position of the thing in the bushes. It has stopped running now, and is muttering some kind of prayer.

The tip of the crossbow bolt glints in the moonlight as it moves, left an inch, up, right . . . *stop.*

Two sounds happen so quickly, they overlap each other. A *twang* and a *thud.*

Birds burst from their roosts in the trees and flap away from the woods, up into the night sky where the hunter's moon shines.

In the distance, on the horizon, it gleams across the peaks of a mountain range of smoke and fog, lit from within by a thousand, thousand lights.

As the thing in the woods dies, London sleeps on, oblivious.

Chapter One

In which cat burglary is invented.

LAMBETH, SOUTH LONDON

'You thievin' little snot-weasels! When we get hold of you, we're going to skin you like rabbits!'

The shout rang out through the courtyard, bouncing back and forth between the crumbling brick buildings that surrounded it and getting lost in the thick grey fog. It was impossible to tell what direction the man was coming from, how close he was, even.

Inji crouched inside a narrow gap between a flight of stone stairs and a pile of steaming rubbish. Horse manure and rotten vegetables, mostly, although there was a shape sticking out of the top that looked like it might be a dead dog's paw. She didn't look closely enough to make certain.

Somewhere in the fog was her brother Sil. Him and a whole group of Lambeth Lads, the gang they had just stolen a very precious item from. Sil was holding that precious thing right now, and probably doing something extremely stupid, like standing out there in the open, trying to catch the fog on his tongue.

He did things like that, if Inji wasn't there to look after him, which is why she never normally left his side. Except now they had got separated, what with all the running and chasing and screaming. That and this gloopy grey mist that stopped you from seeing your hand in front of your face.

The burglary itself had been fine. They had found the Lads' hideout, just where Skinker said it would be. They had lifted up the loose floorboards and found the safe – no problem. They had even used the combination Glyph gave them to open the lockbox first time. Sweet.

It was when they were leaving the place, robbery accomplished, that they bumped into half the gang returning (from a gin shop, judging by the smell). Inji didn't know why they were called 'Lads'. Every one of them was at least twenty, and looked like he had spent nineteen of those years being repeatedly punched in the face.

Their first reaction at seeing Inji and Sil was to scream. To be fair, that's what most people did and Inji couldn't really blame them. But they recovered quicker than average, and also happened to spot the leather bag Sil was holding delicately, as if it contained the Crown Jewels.

Perhaps she shouldn't have told him that's what was in it. He *did* have a tendency to believe everything she said.

'What the jibbering heck?' one of the Lads had said. The biggest one, with the ugliest face. 'That's my blooming bag, that is!'

There had been a pause, then, with the burglars and the burgled staring at each other, as if to say *what a terribly awkward situation, chaps!*

Inji had been the first to break it, by grabbing Sil's arm and screaming, 'Run!' Then they had turned tail, back past the hideout, down some stairs and into the street. Feet sliding on cobbles, screams behind them: but somewhere along the line she had got separated from her brother and the fog had swirled into the gap, hiding him completely.

Now she was in the courtyard, waiting to be found and skinned alive.

'I know you're in here, you hairy sneak!'

Damn, Inji thought. She'd been hoping the Lads had been too shocked to look at her closely. Too surprised to notice how her skin was covered with fine fur – delicately striped – how her ears narrowed to points that jutted out of her tangled brown hair, and how the pupils of her eyes were slitted like a cat.

Stupid of her, she supposed, but now they would know exactly who'd sent them. There was only one gang in the underworld of London that had a bunch of sideshow acts in it, and that was Tannikin Skinker's. As criminals themselves, the Lads would know that. *We've been rumbled*, she chided herself, *and if we ever get out of this, we're in for another hiding when we get home.*

'They've gone in 'ere!' the voice shouted again, and this time Inji could see the rough shape of a figure: a grey shadow blocking the only entrance to the slum courtyard. 'Nobby! Chalky! They're in this 'ere rookery![i] Bring your barkers!'

Barkers. Inji shuddered. That meant pistols. Whatever they'd stolen was valuable enough to be killed for. She had to find Sil and get out of there *now.*

One of the – very few – bonuses of having as much cat blood as human was that her senses were sharper than anyone else's. Sight, smell, hearing: Inji's were all like razors. Especially at times like these, when she was frightened or angry. The cat inside her head wanted to take over, then. She could feel it now, yowling and yammering behind her eyeballs.

Careful to keep it under control, she relaxed her grip a fraction, letting her feline side edge out. She felt the fur all over her body bristle, winced as the curved claws in her fingertips popped their sheaths. A hiss and a yowl built up in her throat. Somehow she managed to keep them there.

With the changes to her body came a boost to her senses. The fog seemed to thin a little. The smell of the dead dog in his horse-dung grave grew regrettably stronger.

And there, in a corner of the slum courtyard,

tongue out to catch the fog droplets, was her twin brother.

The Lad at the entrance hadn't seen him yet, but he would soon, when his mates arrived. Inji reckoned she had a handful of heartbeats to get to Sil and scarper before they both became target practice for the Lambeth Uglies.

Keeping low to the ground, slinking like only she could slink, Inji made her way around the edge of the courtyard, praying hard to whatever god or saint protected sideshow orphans. If there even was one.

For Sil was as strange as her, albeit in another way. For whatever reason (their mother had been a Romany gypsy, and was convinced it was a curse), they had both been born . . . different. Inji had come out looking half kitten. Sil had to be cut free, almost killing their ma. He looked like . . . well, there were no words for it. Not until the day Inji had seen a stuffed armadillo in a curiosity shop and called her twin over to look at it.

That, she'd said. *That is what you look like, brother!*

Where Inji was covered with short, silky fur,

Sil's skin was stretched over knobbled flaps of armour. His hide was as thick as bone, and his head was too. He didn't think or move too quickly, did Sil. And if Inji wasn't there to guide him, he would probably wander off under a horse and cart, or into the Thames itself, to drown in the black rotten mud.

Slink, slink, she slipped soundlessly between piles of rags and puddles of sewage. Keeping to the shadows, wrapped deep in the fog, she reached her brother without the Lad spotting her. His friends were getting closer now: she could hear their feet pounding the cobbles of the street outside.

'Sil!' she whispered. It came out as the hissing spit of an angry mog. 'Sil! What are you doing?'

She was close enough to see his face now. Those wide brown eyes, full of innocence and lost in their own special world. They blinked at her from under the heavy bone ridge of his brow.

'Give me that.' Inji snatched the leather satchel from him. Normally, she would have felt bad about the hurt look on his face, but now the cat was in control, and cats didn't care about things like feelings.

'I 'eard a voice!' the Lad shouted, stepping into the courtyard now. Another silhouette joined him, this one holding something out in one hand. Something very gunlike.

Inji hissed again. The cat was close to the surface now. If she let it loose, it would probably run up and over the rooftops in a flash of brown fur. Escape for her – death for Sil.

The rooftops, though . . .

Inji focused, holding the feline urges in check, looking deep into her brother's eyes. 'Sil, do you remember that time in the workhouse? That time you climbed?'

Their mother had died in the workhouse.[ii] Locked up for being a homeless vagrant after she'd left her Romany community. Her children had been locked up too, although they were only four years old. As soon as their mother wasn't there to protect them, they had been beaten and bullied by staff and inmates alike. Everyone in the place feared and hated them, so they had simply scaled the walls and escaped.

'Climb?' Sil said. He rarely spoke, and when he did it was quite loud. Inji winced.

'There! In the corner!' There was a *bang* that made her head ring, and a window to the left of them smashed.

'Yes, Sil! Climb! Climb now!'

Trusting that he would follow, Inji clutched the satchel in her mouth and sprang up to the wall. Her clawed fingers dug into the crumbling brick like it was stale sponge cake, and she leapt in a series of catlike bounds, straight up the vertical surface to the roof above.

The slum building was tiled with loose, mossy slates, and for a moment she scrabbled at the roof edge, tiles spinning loose to smash on the courtyard cobbles behind her.

There was another gunshot – *crack!* – a slate beside her shattered, and then she was up, over the edge, skittering up the slanted roof to safety. Clinging to the ridgepole, she heard a rhythmic crunching sound, and seconds later, Sil appeared.

His armoured body was amazingly strong. Just like in the workhouse, six long years ago, he had climbed the building by punching his own handholds. He smashed holes in the roof now too, pulling himself up and over. There was a final gunshot, the

bullet actually bouncing off Sil's armoured back and tearing the oversized jacket that covered it, and then they were both safely out of range.

'We know who your boss is!' came a shout from below. 'Tell Skinker he's a dead man!'

But they were high above the Lambeth Lads now. The sea of rooftops that was the London skyline stretched out before them, rising from the waves of grey fog that choked the streets. From up here they could travel most of the way back to the river without even touching the ground, and then it was a short trot across London Bridge, back to the East End.

Back to a hiding from Skinker, when he finds out we were seen, Inji reminded herself, but right now she found it hard to care.

She gave Sil a swift hug, and then took his hand, pulling him along on their rooftop journey.

*

The walk back to Whitechapel took up a good two hours. Sil tended to move at a slow, waddling pace, shifting his bulk from side to side. He also liked to stop quite often, fascinated by tiny things that

Inji would normally never have noticed. The drops of mist caught in a cobweb, or a certain pattern of brickwork. He loved the different chimney pots up high, and cooed over funny-shaped ones, tracing the trails of smoke with his finger.

They found a wooden staircase and clambered down to street level. Inji had an old shawl tied around her waist that she used to drape over herself when she was out in public. Sil's jacket had a hood, which hid his lumpy head. He still looked a funny shape, but people with hunched backs or twisted spines weren't that uncommon on the streets. At worst, he got shouted at to walk faster, but most folk just ignored him.

It hadn't always been that way. After escaping the workhouse, they had only lasted a few months on the streets before some enterprising cove sold them off to a sideshow master.[iii] They had performed almost every night after that. *The Monster Twins* was their most popular name, although they had also been known as *Cat Girl and Armadillo Boy, The Devil's Spawn* and, Inji's least favourite, *The Gargoyle Family.*

About a year ago they had been 'rescued' by their

current boss, Tannikin Skinker, who had found a new use for their talents: stealing things.

From sideshow act to criminal. Inji didn't know which was worse.

They headed for London Bridge and made their way across it to the north bank, keeping a careful eye out for any of the Lambeth Lads who might have tried to intercept them. It was early evening, and there was a flow of workers coming from the East End, back from the docks and factories to their homes. Inji and Sil were buffeted from side to side and crushed up against the stonework more than once, but both of them were used to it.

Off the bridge, they walked up towards Fenchurch Street and then on to Whitechapel Road. The gaslights were just being lit, although the fog seemed to be getting worse, so they didn't do much except make shiny haloes in the gloom. A steady stream of carriages clopped their way along the road; the smell of fresh dung and a barrage of shouting made Inji's head swim. She wished she was back up on the rooftops again, with this world of noise and stink churning away below her.

Along Commercial Street next, until they reached

the tall white spire of Hawksmoor's church. It stretched away, up and up, breaking through the fog, its stone skin becoming cleaner the further it got from the stinking streets. Somewhere above, in the darkening sky, the gold cross on top would be gleaming in the last of the day's sunlight.

Next door, the Ten Bells pub was in full swing, and there were gin-swilling men, women and children spilling out into the street, singing, pushing and swearing. Ducking and barging through them, Inji and Sil headed down Church Street until they came to a ramshackle townhouse with soot-smeared windows.

Looking both ways to check the coast was clear, Inji gave the secret knock and stood back as the door inched open.

A bloodshot eye appeared at the crack, rolling to and fro underneath a wiry eyebrow. A long, hooked nose poked out beneath, nostrils flaring, and under that a wispy ginger beard, stained with rum and tobacco.

'What's this?' the face said. 'What's this at my door?'

'It's us, Tannikin,' said Inji, as if that wasn't

perfectly obvious. 'We've got the goods. Please let us in. It's been a long day.'

The door swung wide, exposing a long, gaslit hallway and a stooped old man in a filthy smoking jacket. He grinned and beckoned at them, giggling and laughing like a child.

'Of course it's you, my bonny little buttons! Old Uncle Tannikin was only joking! Only joshing with you. As if I wouldn't recognise my two finest snatchers! As if *you* two creatures could be mistaken for anyone else on God's green earth.' They stepped over the threshold and he let the door slam behind them. 'Besides,' he added, 'Glyph told me you was coming half an hour ago.'

Tannikin, their boss, their 'saviour', stood before them, rubbing his hands together and shuffling from one foot to the other. His quick grey eyes darted from their faces to the leather satchel and back again.

Ignoring his excitement, Inji took her time about removing her shawl and retying it around her waist. She watched him out of the corner of her eye, trying to judge what mood he was in, and when would be best to tell him they'd been spotted. Exactly when she revealed it would have an important effect on how hard and long he beat them.

'Well?' He couldn't wait any longer. 'Well?'

He really is a disgusting old man, Inji thought. Apart from the layers of filth and dried food all over his jacket and the ancient, stained shirt beneath, he had a gaping hole in the side of his left cheek. He'd worked in a match factory when he was a young man, and suffered a bad case of 'phossy jaw'. The phosphorus in the match heads had eaten away the bone and flesh of his face. Now you could see his back teeth and tongue, gnashing and dribbling as he stared at them. *He's probably the only person in London that looks worse than us.*

'Yes, we got it,' she said, handing him the leather satchel.

Tannikin whooped and cheered like a boy on Christmas Day, dancing a happy jig round and round on the spot. Then he trotted off down the hallway, leaving Inji and Sil to follow.

'Oh, you clever little buttons!' Tannikin sang, waving the bag over his head. 'You sweet little burglar-muffins!'

He led them down the bare hallway to a meagre kitchen, where several oil lamps were flickering, and a pan of some kind of stew simmered on the range. There was a rickety old table, its legs propped up with books, and a selection of threadbare armchairs and stools around it. It was covered in piles of dirty crockery, most of it so chipped and cracked that strands of dried food were all that held it together. Lying open was an evening newspaper, which instantly caught Inji's eye. She had been following a certain case in the papers with great interest. One that Skinker wasn't too keen on her reading about. But before she could look closer, Tannikin snatched the paper and balled it up, throwing it out of sight under the table. He set the satchel down in its place, before taking a chair, still clapping his hands with glee.

Inji pulled a stool across and sat too, trying to keep out of striking distance, still waiting for her chance to break the news. She could see a glimpse of the crumpled paper from where she sat, but not well enough to get a clue what the headline might be. Obviously, it was about the story Skinker wanted to keep from her. *Later, maybe.*

Sil shuffled over to the far wall and sat on a heap of old hessian sacks. The pile instantly began to writhe and wriggle, until a small boy crawled out.

He was dressed in an undersized velvet suit at least twenty years older than him. He had light brown skin, huge dark eyes and a frizzy mop of black hair that zinged out around his head in a crazy cloud. He blinked up at Sil, who blinked back, then reached out a thick-fingered hand to pat him on the head.

'Hello, Glyph,' said Inji. The boy didn't reply, just pulled out a deck of crumpled pasteboard cards from his jacket pocket and began to place them, one by one, on the bare kitchen floorboards, dealing from the top.

Fnap, fnap, fnap.

Inji waited for him to finish and sit back, then she craned her head to see the cards. Instead of suits and numbers, each was printed with a single letter. He had laid out the exact cards needed to spell HELLO.

Glyph was different from other people, like them. But though he looked normal – apart from the desperate need for a haircut – he never spoke, or even made a sound. Instead, the cards talked for him. He dealt them out, always from the top, never seeming to peek, and yet always had the exact ones he needed to spell out his messages.

He could even discover secrets, like he was seeing inside your head. Skinker loved him because he could deal out the combination codes for safes and lockboxes, hidden away and stuffed with valuables. *No lock in London can cheat me*, the warped old crook used to say, whenever he had Glyph dealing out the cards, and Inji supposed he was right.

'Well, then,' said the man himself, jolting Inji back to the present. 'Let's have a little look here, shall we?'

Inji took a deep breath. Now was best, when the pleasure of peeping in the bag might lighten his mood a bit. 'Skinker. Before you do, there's something you should know.'

The old man paused, hooked fingers hanging over the satchel. He glared at Inji, one eyelid beginning to twitch. 'Yes, button?'

'The Lambeth Lads.' She breathed hard again. 'They saw us lifting the goods. They know it was you what sent us.'

Skinker remained frozen for a moment more, that eyelid jittering like a dancing flea. Inji could hear his teeth begin to grind through that hole in his cheek. She started to wince, waiting for the first blow to come, but it didn't. The old man let out a breath and, for the first time since he'd bought them, seemed to master his temper.

'No matter, button, no matter.' He actually gave a laugh, reaching his long, stained fingers into the satchel and pulling out a stack of papers. Cards or etchings, maybe. 'I was going to have to speak to them anyway, wasn't I? Otherwise I'd never be able to get them to pay for the safe return of *these*.'

He began flicking through the cards, the smile on his face growing bigger with each one. By the time he reached the end of the stack, he was howling with laughter, tears spilling down his sunken cheeks.

Inji blinked at him in confusion. She tried to glimpse what was so funny. It was a pile of tintype photographs, with groups of children on.[iv] Perfectly normal kiddies, in sailor suits and bonnets, from what she could see.

Skinker saw her looking, and flipped the top photograph around so she could view it properly. Children, indeed, but very ugly ones. Big-boned, stoop-shouldered, with flat noses and ... *whiskers*?

Inji peered closer. That boy in the middle, with the peaked cap and teddy bear. Was that the leader of the Lambeth Lads dressed up?

'What d'you think, eh?' Skinker slapped the table in glee, making the piles of crockery jump and clink. 'Should call themselves the Lambeth *Littlies*, shouldn't they? Oh my trousers, what they'll pay to get *these* back!'

'How did you know . . .' Inji began, gobsmacked. 'How did you know they did *that*?'

Skinker took a crusty kerchief from a pocket and mopped his eyes. 'Heard a rumour or two, didn't I?' he said. 'Paid a few shillings here and there. Found an old member with an axe to grind that told me where the photos was hid. The roughest gang in South London, dressing up like kidlings for a spot of fun. Who'd have thought it?'

Who'd have thought it indeed? Inji didn't know what to be more surprised about: the Lads' secret pastime, or the fact Skinker hadn't beaten them.

'Good job, good job, my bonny buttons.' Skinker got up now, taking three bowls from the pile and going over to the stove. He spooned some watery stew into them, and then handed them out to Inji, Sil and Glyph.

'You've earned yourselves a hot dinner and a good night's sleep,' he said, smiling in his horrific way. 'Old Uncle Tannikin is off to hide these beauties somewhere safe, and then it's beddy-byes for all of us, don't you think?'

He watched as Sil slurped greedily from the bowl, while Glyph took delicate little sips. Inji hunted in the dirty crockery for a spoon, one eye on the crumpled newspaper under the table. 'G'night, Tannikin,' she said, mentally urging him out of the room.

Instead of speaking, he gave her a quiet, funny look. One she hadn't seen before. If she hadn't been so intent on reading that newspaper, she might have thought more of it, but it went unnoticed. Skinker shuffled off, leaving the three urchins to their supper.

*

Inji waited until she'd heard his footsteps go up the stairs. Skinker's quarters were up there. Properly furnished, she imagined, with actual chairs, tables and beds. She'd never been there, and didn't want to, really. He sometimes had other – normal – members of his gang about. Them and other crooks he worked with. The place for freaks was clearly understood to be downstairs, out of sight.

She fished the crumpled newspaper out from under the table. She began to flatten it, when she noticed Sil had stopped slurping, and was falling asleep sitting up, empty bowl still in hand.

She went over, took the chipped stew bowl away and laid him down on the sacking as best she could. She pulled a bit of hessian over him for a blanket, and smoothed the thin strands of brown hair down on top of his ridged, bony head.

'Sleep tight, brother,' she said, kissing him gently. He usually liked her to sing to him – one of the Romany lullabies their mother had taught them – but all that climbing and walking must have tired him out.

Glyph's eyes were beginning to droop as well. Inji took his bowl too, and helped wrap him in some sacking.

'Are you warm enough there?'

He still had enough energy to reach for his cards.

Fnap, fnap, fnap. Y-E-S.

'Night night, then.' She didn't know Glyph well enough for a goodnight kiss, although she had taken him under her wing almost immediately. Like a proper Mother Hen. Or Mother Cat.

He'd been at Skinker's when they got there. Bought from a fortune teller in Covent Garden, or so she'd heard. Apparently, he'd been living on the streets with his ma – a poor wretch cast out from the house where she'd worked as a maid – until she'd died of something nasty. Neither Glyph nor Skinker knew who his father was. Chances were he was the top man of the posh house where his mum had worked. That kind of thing happened all the time. One of the sad, sad stories that Whitechapel was filled with.

Satisfied they were both sound asleep, Inji returned to her paper.

It was that evening's *Standard*, and only slightly dribbled on by Skinker. She pored over it while she spooned tasteless mutton and cabbage stew into her mouth.

The story she was looking for was halfway down the front page. A new development in the tale she had been following for weeks. 'Another Sideshow Act Murdered', it read, accompanied by a rushed drawing of a masked figure. Inji didn't have a strong grasp of letters, but she had been taught some by

Elspeth, the bearded lady from a show she'd been part of. She knew enough to get the gist, and what she worked out wasn't good.

This was the third murder of its kind in the city in the past few months. All sideshow players and all found dead, pierced through with one or more arrows or bolts that the police thought had been fired from a crossbow.

The first had been a tall man, seven foot six, kidnapped from his lodgings and discovered at the edge of Hyde Park. The second, a minuscule lady 'the size of an elf'. She'd had no fewer than ten bolts in her, and had been found floating in the river.

This one was a contortionist (it took Inji several minutes to read *that* word), which she remembered was someone who could bend their body in unusual ways. There had been one at their show who could fit himself inside a tiny wooden box.

This particular player had been found by the pond in St James's Park. Witnesses had seen a horse and cart pull up, and a masked figure get out to dump the body. The murderer had been dressed in hunting leathers, with a wolf-eared mask and a pair of goggles with smoked-glass lenses.

Some brave soul had asked what he was doing, and the masked man had replied, 'Compliments of the Hunters' Club,' before driving off into the fog.

The Hunters' Club. Inji thought about this as she chewed a stringy piece of mutton. That meant there must be more than one of them. A whole group, maybe, killing sideshow acts as if they were wild deer or pheasants.

We could be next, she thought. Technically, none of them was part of a show, but they all had been, once. And much more unusual acts than those who'd been killed so far. The thought of one madman doing it had been terrifying, which was why Skinker had been hiding the paper from her, but a whole *club* of them?

She looked over to where Sil and Glyph lay sleeping, both of them the picture of innocence. A fierce rush of protective anger washed over her, and she felt her fur bristle and a hiss pop from her throat.

Let them try and take one of us, she thought. *I'll scratch their eyes out. Even if there is more than one. I'll teach them to leave our kind alone. As if our lives haven't been hard enough already.*

She looked at the picture again, taking in the wolf mask and goggles. At least now she had an idea of what the villains looked like.

As she stared, she found her own eyes were beginning to droop shut. She hadn't thought she was so tired.

So *very* tired.

Her head swam, and the paper blurred in and out of focus. This wasn't normal sleepiness, she realised. She must have eaten or drunk a drug, some kind of poison . . .

The stew! Skinker must have drugged the mutton stew! Sil and Glyph were out cold and soon she would be too.

Stop . . . eating . . . but her bowl was half empty already, her stomach full of the stuff.

She had time for one thought, just before her head fell on the table.

Why, Skinker?

Why?

CHAPTER TWO

In which our heroes meet the hunter.

D*ark. Wrists bound. Can't move.* Inji opened her eyes. They were heavy, gritty. Her head felt like someone had stuffed it with sawdust, then used it as a football for an hour or two.

Wood, fresh-cut. She could smell timber and feel it underneath her, to her right *and* above. A glimmer of light crept in through a knothole, not far from her head. From the colour and quality, she guessed it was gaslight from a street lamp. She was outside, then, trapped in a box or crate.

'Sil? Glyph?' Something soft and warm pressed up against her left side. She guessed it was one of them. Listening closely, she could hear Sil's burbling breath as he slept, and another, lighter snore. The pair of them must be in the crate with her. They had finished off their stew completely, she remembered, while she had only eaten half of hers.

Skinker.

He had drugged them, bound them and boxed them. Why? He was a mean, violent crook, true, but he made good money out of them. Had they annoyed him somehow? Had he received a better offer?

His funny mood that evening made perfect sense now. Why beat the goods he was about to part with?

It made Inji angry, and with anger came the cat. *Loose me!* it cried. *Let me scratch my way out!*

'Later,' Inji promised it. She might need its strength and ferocity, but for now she had to discover more about their predicament.

The knothole. By shuffling herself over to the right and pressing her nose up against the boards, she was able to get an eye to the hole. They were outside all right, in the street by Skinker's lair. It was full night now, still foggy, but her feline night vision made everything shine clear. There was a gaslight nearby, and there: Skinker's front door.

She could hear voices, just a few feet away, and

the whickering of horses. They must have been loaded on to a cart, ready to be taken somewhere.

Not if I have anything to do with it, she thought. She sucked in a lungful of air and yelled.

'Skinker! Skinker, you ugly, cheekless, beardy weasel!'

The voices stopped. Whoever it was had heard her. She tried again.

'Skinker, let us out! Let us out of here, or I'll scratch off the rest of your face. That's a promise!'

There was a shuffling of slippered feet on paving stones, and a hunched form appeared out of the fog. It was Skinker himself, staring up at the crate and smiling one of his crazed grins.

'Now, now, button. No need to be so cross.' His eyes moved back and forth, probably checking the crate was sealed properly. He obviously hadn't expected any of them to be awake.

'What are you doing with us? Why are we in here?'

In answer, Skinker held up a leather purse and shook it. Inji could hear the clinking of a great many coins inside. Gold ones, probably. 'It breaks my heart, button, but I had an offer I couldn't refuse. This nice man has paid more for you than you could ever earn, I'm afraid.'

'Who? Who's paid for us?'

Skinker laughed at this, and beckoned to someone just out of her sight. 'Well, button – and this is a funny coincidence and no mistake – you know those murdered sideshow acts you've been so interested in lately? It just so happens, your new owner is none other than . . . the culprit himself!'

At this, a second man appeared. He was tall, dwarfing Skinker, broad and dressed in a padded leather coat and trousers. Inji stared through the knothole, trying to see his face, and was horrified when she realised she couldn't. She couldn't because he was masked in animal fur, with a pair of smoked-glass goggles.

The Hunters' Club.

Inji screamed then, and let the cat have full control. She hissed, yowled and hammered at the crate. She kicked with her tied feet. Her claws dug gouges and splinters, but with her wrists bound, they had little effect.

Outside, she could hear Skinker laughing, and the hunter talking to the horses. There was a jolt, and the cart began to move, bumping up and down on the cobbles.

Somehow, Inji's eye found the knothole again, and she saw a crowd had gathered at all the commotion. Skinker was shooing them away, but there was a boy staring up, eyes wide with terror, and his fingers – hooked over the edges of his pockets – they were much longer than normal fingers should be. Was he *different* too, like them?

'Help!' Inji screamed at him. 'Help us! Kidnap! Murder!'

The boy shouted something back, and then disappeared into the throng. Inji hadn't heard exactly what he said, but it sounded like – she prayed it was – *I'll get help!*

*

The cart bumped its way through the city, rattling over the cobbles and shaking Inji about like a rag doll in a puppy's mouth.

She tried to keep her eye at the knothole as much as she could, but it was difficult when they were moving. Luckily, this part of London was busy through most of the night, so they had to stop frequently. Whenever the horses halted, she rammed her eye to the hole and tried to get her bearings.

First they headed up Brick Lane, northwards, then turned to the right, to the east. Now they were moving through Bethnal Green. Inji could see all the crumbling slum houses beside the road, huddled forms sleeping in doorways, or stumbling down the street. Every now and then there was a child, a scruffy street urchin, running along beside the cart. At first, Inji thought it might be the same boy that she'd shouted to outside Skinker's, but the next one was a girl, and another time two children together. All showed glimpses of unusual features: the flash of a tail, the flutter of tiny wings. Or at least Inji thought they did. Perhaps her terrified mind was playing tricks on her. They chased the cart for a bit, then darted off down an alley or side street.

Just homeless street children, playing silly games when they should be asleep, Inji thought. *Don't get your hopes up.*

She shouted out to some of the passers-by she saw, but her voice was hoarse now, and if they heard they didn't even bat an eyelid. You could quite literally be murdered on the street in this part of town, and people would just give you a cheerful wave as they strolled by.

Her only chance, she thought, was to wake Sil somehow. He was strong enough to punch through the wooden box like it was made of brown paper. Then she'd have a chance at that Hunters' Club cove. He was probably armed, but that wouldn't be enough to save him from a ball of scratching, hissing catgirl fury.

Except Sil wouldn't stir. Whatever Skinker had given them, it was strong stuff. She nudged him, poked him, even tried to butt him with her head. All that did was give her forehead a bruise and made stars sparkle in front of her eyes. That boy's bone armour was *tough.*

Maybe there was nothing she could do. Maybe they just had to wait until they got wherever they were being taken.

Would the hunters let them out first, or just shoot their crossbow bolts straight into the wooden crate? *Wouldn't be much of a hunt if they did that.* Perhaps they would untie them and let them run a bit before the shooting started. Sil and Glyph would have to be awake for that to work. That suggested their captors might be going to keep them somewhere, at least for a bit. Might it be a place they could escape from? She and Sil were good at that. And with Glyph to give them some hints with his cards . . .

Inji began to feel a glimmer of hope. Not much: just a gnat's eyebrow, maybe, but at least it was there.

The cart stopped again, and she shuffled over to peep out of the hole. They were on Hackney Road now, still heading north. If they went much further, they would be out of Inji's familiar territory, and she'd have no idea where they were.

She looked around for anyone who wasn't drunk or asleep – anyone who might help. Another little form scurried past, darting into a gap between two buildings. This one had a covering of hedgehog prickles all over its scalp.

'Hey!' Inji shouted, although it came out more of a croak. 'Don't go! Help!'

'Be quiet, back there!' It was the first time she had clearly heard the hunter speak. His voice was deep – posh-sounding. Like someone who should be out sipping sherry at a gentlemen's club, instead of carting kidnapped children around crumbling, foggy slums.

'Why don't you come here and try shutting me

up?' Inji tried to sound brave, but her voice shook a little. This wasn't Skinker and his broom handle she was facing up to. This bloke was a killer, and he probably had at least a dagger on him. Maybe worse.

'I will if you don't . . .' The hunter never finished his sentence. Inji heard the sound of something smacking into him, and a grunt followed by a retch of disgust. She jumped as another missile hit her crate with a loud bang. It was followed a second after by one of the worst things she had ever smelt. Like a scoop from an overflowing privy on a hot summer's day, swilled around in the skull of a dead rat.

'Eat stink, you leather-bound foozler!' a voice shouted from somewhere down the road.

The hunter cried out again, and the smell got worse. Someone was pelting him with fresh dog droppings, or some other sort of dung. Inji stuck her eye to the knothole, trying to see who it was.

Blam! A gunshot rang out, echoing off the walls all around them. The few homeless people she could see on the pavements quickly gathered up their rags and blankets and began to run for cover.

'Missed me, you fart in a leather overcoat! Call

yourself a hunter? You couldn't hit . . .'

Blam!

'Oi! Watch out! That was nearly my elbow!'

Elbow? Whoever it was, they were clearly mad, and they were also going to get themselves killed. Poo-balls against a pistol wasn't a fair fight.

Then the crate shook as somebody landed on it. A soft landing, graceful, but enough to rock the cart. Inji heard hands and feet pad across the wood, inches above her nose. And a scraping sound too – almost like claws?

Blam! BLAM!

If only her rescuers could keep the hunter firing, the police – the crushers – would be here soon enough. That's if there were any about in this part of town. Inji strained her ears to hear police whistles going off. Instead, there was a low growling, like an angry dog. One who's just about to bite your face off.

'Show yourself, you blackguard!' the hunter was shouting, his clipped Eton accent more obvious than ever. The poo thrower must have run out of ammo. Either that or he'd been hit.

Scratch, scratch. The thing on top of the crate

moved closer to the driver. He was so intent on spotting his target, he hadn't thought to look behind him. Inji heard a sudden loud snarl, then the crate shook as the thing on top launched itself through the air. A high-pitched yell of terror followed, then a *thud* as someone fell from the cart and hit the cobbles.

Inji heard the clatter of a metallic object skittering away across the stones – *the gun*, she thought – and then there was lots of tearing, gnashing and screaming. It reminded her of a dog fight she had seen once, when she was living on the streets with Sil. She had only been tiny, but those feral, vicious sounds could never be forgotten.

To her relief, it only went on for a few seconds. The hunter must have escaped the dog, wolf, or whatever it was, and then run off down the street. She heard his pounding footsteps fade away, although she could still smell hot, coppery blood.

There was silence for a good minute or two after that.

Inji lay there, bound in the dark, wondering what had just happened. Were they safe? Were they free? Or had they just been kidnapped again by someone even worse than the Hunters' Club?

The answer came a few seconds later. She heard the poo-ball thrower's voice again: 'Are you all right, Sheba? I thought you were going to wait until he was out of bullets? He didn't hit you, did he?'

And then a woman speaking: gasping words as though she were out of breath. 'No. No, I don't think so. I was going to wait, but then the wolf . . .'

'Ah. Hard to control still? I thought you were going to have that man for supper, there.'

'I was trying not to. I had to hold it back, but then the man escaped. Our best chance, gone . . .'

'Don't worry, Sheba. It isn't a complete disaster. He left the crate, after all. Shall we see what's inside?'

The cart lurched as somebody clambered aboard, and then there was a wrenching, splintering sound as a crowbar was shoved under the wooden lid and levered up and down.

Hurry, hurry, Inji thought, desperate to be out of the box, to have her arms and legs free again.

There was a final *crunch* and the lid creaked open, revealing grey, gaslit fog above, and a shadow of the moon, weakly shining through. Inji looked up, trying to get a glimpse of her rescuer. Would it be a masked man again? Or a brutish gang member?

Another sideshow boss? A murdering villain?

What she saw was a monster.

A man-sized creature, with oversized arms and hands like giant spiders. He had a mouth full of crooked fangs and a pair of wide yellow eyes, glowing like a pair of lanterns.

'Bless my mutton chops,' he said. 'I never thought I'd find someone in London that looked weirder than me, and then a whole bunch of 'em come along at once!'

Chapter Three

In which Inji discovers kindness . . . and cocoa.

A few minutes later, Inji found herself in their rescuers' own carriage.

The monster-faced man had helped her lift Sil ('Gorblimey, he weighs more than a pregnant elephant!') and Glyph out of the crate, and drag them into the vehicle. They now lay side by side on the seat next to her, still dead to the world.

The man had then jumped up to the driver's board outside, leaving Inji to climb in, along with the young lady whose voice she had heard. Of the dog, or wolf, or whatever it was, no sign could be seen.

'Are you all right?' the lady asked her now.

'Would you like some water?'

Inji shook her head. She hadn't really paid much attention to this woman, what with all the lifting and shoving of Glyph and her brother. Now she snuck some sly glances while pretending to look around the carriage.

She was quite young – eighteen or nineteen maybe – and very pretty. She had smooth, pale skin, chestnut-brown hair that hung in shiny curls around her shoulders, and a button of a nose. Her lips were full, and twitched into a friendly smile every time she glanced at Inji. She was wearing a loose black shirt that had tears at the shoulders, her pale skin peeping through. And *trousers* too! Inji had never seen a posh young lady in trousers, even though she wore them herself.

But the most striking thing about her was her eyes. Heavy-lidded, with long lashes, they seemed to be deep orange in colour, like polished amber. Except every now and then, when the carriage passed through a building's shadow and the inside darkened, they glowed. As if a secret light was burning inside them.

Inji had never seen anything like it. It made her

wonder, just for a second, if perhaps the wolf who attacked the hunter and the beautiful young woman opposite her might be the same creature. A crazy thought, maybe, but if she had a wildcat sharing her body, why couldn't other people be the same?

Inji peered closer at the perfect skin of her face, trying to spot any hair.

'I'm Sheba, by the way,' said the lady, making Inji jump. 'What's your name?'

'Inji.' She wished she had accepted some water. Her voice was croaky from all the screaming and hissing. 'Where are we going?'

'We are going back to our house,' said Sheba. 'You can rest there, and eat. Perhaps we have medicine that can wake your friends. They seem to have been drugged quite deeply. After that, we would like to ask you a few questions, and then we can return you to your home?'

She raised her voice, like it was an option. Inji fiercely shook her head. She was never going back to Skinker's. Not ever.

'Or perhaps we can find you somewhere else to stay.' Something in the lady's eyes seemed to say *I understand.* But how could she? How could anyone 'normal' have *any* idea of what it was like to be bought and sold like a slave? To be put on show: stared at by laughing punters, or made to creep through the night, stealing things, for a boss who was as likely to beat you with a stick as feed you?

Just thinking about it made Inji fume. She decided to change the subject before she lost control of herself and scratched up the carriage's lovely leather interior.

'What questions?'

'Just some questions regarding the man who was taking you. Nothing about you or your friends. Don't worry.'

'Why?' Inji couldn't help being curious (even though that kind of thing was very bad for cats). 'Why d'you want to know about *him*?'

Sheba paused for a moment, choosing her words. 'My friend Pyewacket and I – we're ... investigators.'

'Like the Pinkertons?' Inji had read about them in the paper. The Pinkerton Agency were detectives from America. People whose job was to sneak around, catching criminals and solving cases. A bit like the peelers, but without the silly hats and the whistles. It had always sounded exciting to Inji, and a career she thought she'd be quite good at herself, seeing as how sneaking about was also her occupation (although it happened to be on the other side of the law).

'Yes, just like them!' Sheba gave her a brilliant smile. Inji noticed what white and ... what *sharp* teeth she had. 'Except we tend to take on cases that are a touch more ... unusual. Involving people like us – "gifted", we call ourselves – mostly. We help out where we can. Try to make the lives of other folk easier. Help them become more ... accepted.'

'Are you investigating *them*, then? The Hunters' Club?'

'So you've heard of them,' said Sheba, her eyes flashing again. 'Yes we are. And we think you might be able to assist us. Did the man say anything to you?'

'I've got a question for you, first,' said Inji, jutting out her chin.

'Certainly.' Sheba sat back, plucking at the torn fabric of her sleeves.

'How did you know we was in that crate? There could have been anything in there. You could have killed that bloke over a box of old potatoes.'

'Ah.' Sheba smiled. 'Well. We were told you were inside. Some young friends of ours spotted you being driven away from Whitechapel. We've been asking them to keep an eye out for anything like that, you see.'

'Those street kids who were following the cart?'

'You spotted them? Very good.'

Inji felt a flush of pride for a second before telling herself not to be stupid. This wasn't a schoolroom. For all she knew this woman and her friend were as bad as the hunters, and all this talk of investigations was a smokescreen.

'Yes,' Sheba continued. 'They were part of the Gutter Brigade, as Pyewacket likes to call them. They've come in useful more than once, keeping their eyes out for us around the city.'

'How does that work, then?' It was the first Inji had heard of such a thing, and it intrigued her. Hidden networks, secret cases. *Careful*, her cat self reminded her, *you still don't know who this pair are, or what they want. Keep your claws ready.*

'It's simple, really,' Sheba was saying. 'There are several children we've had to help, or whose families needed our support. Some we saved from cruel gang bosses, one or two from being worked to death as chimney sweeps. A whole family who were turned out by a nasty landlord. Now they all live together in a tenement on Brick Lane, which I pay the rent for. It keeps them safe but, of course, the children can't go to school like others do. All of them are gifted, you see. So we came up with a way to keep them busy. Each of them has been given a patch, all across London, and they pass messages on to us when they spot clues, one child to another.' She smiled at her invention. 'It's faster than the telegraph.'

There was a clatter from outside, and the vehicle came to a sudden halt, making Sheba and Inji rock in their seats. Pyewacket yelled down from his perch outside: 'We're here!'

With all the talking, Inji hadn't noticed that they'd crossed the river. She could smell it as she climbed out of the carriage and hear the sound of boats clanking up and down, muffled shouts in the fog. That meant Southwark or Bermondsey. Rotherhithe, maybe.

She took a quick look around as Sheba climbed down after her. They were on a narrow, gaslit street, flanked by Georgian townhouses; tall, three- and four-storey brick buildings with rows of long rectangular windows. Deep in the night, nothing moved here but the fog.

'I'll take the carriage round the back,' Pyewacket called down. 'I can bring the sleeping beauties in on my own. You girls go and have a cup of cocoa.' He gave Inji a cheeky wink. 'Or a saucer of milk.'

She was about to tell him where to shove it, but he'd already started to gee the horse on, heading down an alleyway at the side of one of the houses. It was as tall and old as the rest, but looked in better shape. The roof was new, Inji noticed, and the door repainted. A polished brass number 17 stood out against the dark blue. On the wall next to it, a plaque read: *Carnival of the Lost: Private Investigators.*

'Welcome to Paradise Street,' said Sheba, and led the way in.

*

Inji smelt fresh varnish and paste as Sheba opened the door and turned up the gaslights. They walked into a large hallway, decorated with patterned wallpaper and matching rugs over new floorboards.

Framed silhouette portraits and tintype photographs hung on the walls. An umbrella stand held several parasols and a walking cane. It was the poshest house Inji had ever been in.

'This is yours?' she said, wondering to herself why anybody who lived in such luxury would want to be out in the dark, dangerous streets, rescuing kidnapped sideshow acts.

Sheba smiled again, teeth glinting, and opened the door to their right, beckoning Inji into a neat parlour room. 'It is now. It belonged to my parents. Pyewacket and I have been decorating.'

'It's nice,' Inji grunted. 'Smart.'

'Thank you.' Sheba gestured for her to sit. 'If you just wait here a moment, I'll make us some cocoa to have before bed.'

Inji shrugged, trying to seem uninterested, although a part of her wanted to cry with gratitude. Nobody had *ever* been this nice to her. She wondered what Sil and Glyph would make of all this when they woke up. Maybe she should go and find them – make sure that Pyewacket bloke was gently lifting them out of the cab and not throwing them around like sacks of hay?

But some instinct rooted her to her seat. She clutched her hands together, hunched up, not wanting to touch anything for fear of breaking it.

She was perched on a patterned fabric armchair; two others matched it across the room. The far wall had a small fireplace, where coals were gently smouldering, making everything snug and warm.

Polished walnut tables were everywhere: tiny ones by the chairs, a bigger one before the fire and more around the room's edges. They were covered with lace doilies and ornaments: brass figurines, pieces of china. A delicate ebony box sat on the mantelpiece, carved all over with jasmine flowers. Everything was so *tasteful.* Like the rooms she'd glimpsed through windows when roaming the streets on an errand for Skinker. She never thought she'd actually be inside one of those places. Waiting for hot cocoa, of all things.

There were more pictures on the wall. Portraits of a man in red army uniform and a lady in a white silk dress. Sheba's parents? Rich enough to have their pictures painted, and to live in a place like *this*.

And there were more photographs on the other wall. Inji looked closer this time, and her eyes widened in surprise. One was of a group of mismatched figures that couldn't be anything other than the cast of a penny sideshow. She knew, because she'd posed for pictures just the same. Lopsided, mismatched bodies, stone-serious faces that were trying to hide the endless misery of the lives they lived.

It gave her a lurch of some strange new feeling: a mix of horror and nostalgia. She got off her chair and tiptoed closer, filled with fascination, and a touch of guilt at being so nosy.

The group of figures was standing in a yard, gathered before an old gypsy caravan. The kind she half remembered from the days with her mother, before the workhouse.

There were five of them: a huge, muscled strongman, a woman in a broad hat with two rats on her shoulder, a teenage girl with long black hair and dark glasses under a top hat, and two children at the front. One was clearly a younger version of Pyewacket. The other was a little girl, with sharp eyes and long, curled locks. And fur all over her face.

Inji's fingers moved to her own cheeks, feeling the soft hair. If the boy was now the man who'd rescued them, who was this girl? Could she be Sheba? But what had happened to her hairy face?

Next to the tintype was a framed playbill. A cheaply printed bit of yellowed paper, the same type that was plastered in papier-mâché layers over every single wall in the East End.

Carnival of the Lost, it read. *Misfits, Oddments and Monstrosities. Terror and Amazement await you. Entry 1d.*

'*Carnival*,' Inji whispered. Her slitted eyes blinked slowly as she tried to fathom how two sideshow acts like her had ended up in a beautiful house like *this.* Her thoughts were interrupted by footsteps in the hallway, and the chinking sound of cups and saucers being carried. She dashed back to the chair and composed herself as best she could.

Sheba entered a moment later, setting a tray down on one of the side tables and handing Inji a china cup from it. It was full of rich brown cocoa, still steaming. Inji breathed in the chocolatey smell, savouring it. She had smelt the stuff before, from shop doorways, and once or twice when Skinker had served it to his thugs upstairs, but never had a cup been hers.

Sil would love this, she thought, feeling a pang of guilt. From somewhere down the hall she could hear Pyewacket lifting him into the house. She really should go and see if he was all right . . .

'Careful, it's hot,' Sheba said. She had taken a cup herself and was blowing on it, her full lips pursed, her eyes watching Inji intently.

'My brother. And Glyph . . .' Inji started to say.

'They're still fast asleep, but they're fine. Pyewacket is just bringing them inside now. Whatever they were given, they got a good dose.'

A shout came from down the corridor: 'I've got the big one in the kitchen, Sheba, but I'm not blooming carrying him up the stairs. He's given me a hernia already!'

'That's fine,' Inji said quickly. 'He's used to sleeping in a kitchen anyway. If he comes round and things are different . . . Well, he doesn't like change very much.'

'Are you sure?' said Sheba. 'There are spare bedrooms upstairs . . .'

'No. Thank you.' She pictured Sil waking up without her, in a new place. He would cry for sure, maybe lose his temper. Things tended to get broken when he did that. Things like walls and furniture and the bones of anybody who was in the way. 'I'll stay with him too. So I'm the first thing he sees.'

Sheba smiled at her. 'You're a very good sister,' she said, before calling down the corridor to Pyewacket. 'You can leave them in the kitchen, please! Get some blankets, though. Make them comfortable!'

There was the sound of someone stomping up the stairs and slamming cupboard doors, along with lots of muttered curses. Inji took the chance to blow on her cocoa and take a sip. It was delicious: like drinking melted gold.

'It's past midnight,' Sheba said. 'You must be very tired.'

Inji shrugged. Sleeping could wait. More cocoa first. She slurped at her cup.

'Would you mind if I asked you some questions, then?'

Inji stopped slurping and stared at Sheba. What if this woman got what she wanted and then threw them out on the street? It didn't seem like she'd do that, but then all this kindness and cocoa could be an act . . .

'I think I *am* a bit sleepy, actually.' Inji decided to play for time. And at least get a good night's kip beside a warm kitchen fire. Maybe even some of breakfast. 'Although I did have a question for you . . .'

'Yes?'

'Those people in that picture there.' Inji pointed at the sideshow group. 'Who is that young girl?'

Sheba blinked her amber eyes at Inji. This conversation was like two wild animals circling each other, each wondering if the other was trustworthy.

'It is me,' she said finally. 'And there's Pyewacket too. We were part of a sideshow once.'

'How, then . . .?'

'How did we end up here? Well, I found this place when I was eight or so. Although my parents were long gone by then. I never knew them, unfortunately. One of my relatives discovered me. Turned out he's quite important. He made sure I got my inheritance, and this house. Otherwise we would still be there, like as not. Putting on shows and being laughed at.'

'I was in a show too.' Inji hadn't meant to give

anything away, but the words slipped out. To have found someone else with that in common . . .

'Was that where the Hunters' Club took you from?'

'No, that was before. We were sold from it to a crook called Skinker . . .' Inji quickly bit her lip. She was giving too much away. Instead she pressed on with what she *really* wanted to ask. 'In that photograph, though . . . you've got hair on your face. Like . . . like . . .'

'Like you?' Sheba smiled and nodded.

'But your skin is so smooth now.' Inji almost didn't dare speak her next question. 'Does it . . . does it fall out? When you grow up?'

Sheba shook her head. 'Not by itself.' She pointed at the picture again. 'You see this other girl? With the dark glasses? Her name is Sister Moon. She came from Hong Kong, and had all sorts of interesting skills. She showed me how to focus – meditate, is what she called it – and that gave me some control over the wolf part of me. I can tame it now – make it be still. And then the hair doesn't show.'

'Do you think . . .' Inji found she couldn't say the words. The cat in her head was hissing at her.

Her china cup was rattling against the saucer as her hand shook.

'Do I think you could do it too?' Sheba shrugged. 'I don't see why not. I imagine we are similar, you and I. But it takes years of practice and training. It's not a quick solution.'

Not quick, Inji thought, *but there's hope.* 'Is she here now? The girl who taught you?'

Sheba glanced at the picture again, and Inji saw the sadness in her eyes. 'No. She's not.' Sheba sighed. 'Just before I was granted this house, our old sideshow master – a man called Plumpscuttle – sold her to a theatre in Paris. I get the odd letter from her now and then, but it's not the same as having her here . . .'

'And the others?'

'Gigantus and Mama Rat? They left soon after. They joined another . . . *group*, I suppose you'd call it. No, it's just me and Pyewacket now. We decided to stick together, to put our talents to good use. Word soon spread among others like us, and we were able to help some of them. We exposed several cruel masters, found homes for those with no hope. We even solved a murder or two. And here we are.' She sighed again.

'Maybe your old friends will come back,' Inji said. 'Maybe you won't have to be alone. With that rude so-and-so.' She gestured towards the corridor and stuck her tongue out. To her delight, Sheba threw her head back and laughed.

'Maybe they will,' she said. 'But for tonight, it's time to sleep. And in the morning, it will be *my* turn to ask the questions.'

Fair enough, thought Inji. She took a final slurp of cocoa, and then followed Sheba down to the kitchen, every bone in her body suddenly aching for sleep.

Chapter Four

In which Inji and the others find a new home.

Inji woke to the smell of frying bacon. She poked her nose out from the nest of blankets she had made and breathed in the delicious scent of sizzling meat, mixed with that of hot, freshly baked bread.

For a moment, she thought she might have died in that crate after all, and woken up in heaven. Then she put an eye to her blanket-hole and saw Pyewacket at the stove, stirring fat chunks of bacon in a pan of melted butter and quietly humming a tune to himself, his long, hairy arms hanging out of his shirtsleeves.

They were in a neat kitchen, complete with a stove, table and chairs, a large sink with a water pump, and a dresser stacked with a matching set of blue willow-pattern crockery. There was a door to the hallway, another that led outside, and the bottom steps of a servants' staircase in the corner. Morning sunlight streamed in from the large window behind her and gleamed on the spotless whitewashed walls. Time to get up.

It was hard to leave her soft pile of clean, sweet-smelling blankets (so much nicer than the scraps of lice-ridden sacking she was used to), but . . . *bacon.*

Inji wriggled her way out and spent a few moments stretching her back, then one limb after the other, enjoying the almost painful pull of every muscle, and the soft pops of her joints as they unclicked themselves.

Sil was curled up next to her, shrouded in a patchwork quilt. She gave him a nudge, and he began to stir. *Oh no*, she thought. *Quick!* She uncovered his head and moved herself so that her face filled his field of vision. She put her hands on his cheeks, against the nubs of bony tissue that grew there, and rubbed gently, feeling the bumps and ridges beneath his skin, soothing him.

‘Sil?’ She kept her voice soft and quiet. ‘Sil? Are you awake?’

Beneath his lumpy brow, Sil’s eyes popped open. They blinked a few times, recognising his sister, but he could tell something was different. His nose was twitching, taking in the new scents.

Inji kept stroking his face. ‘Sil, don’t panic. Stay calm. We’re not at Skinker’s any more. We’re somewhere else. Somewhere safe, all right?’

She gradually moved aside, so he could see his surroundings, and braced herself for having to jump on him, in case he decided to get angry.

Except he didn’t. He just stared at Pyewacket, or more specifically the skillet in his hands, his mouth watering.

Next to him, Glyph had woken up too. He yawned, shook his head, and then blinked in surprise when he found himself in a different kitchen. When he met Inji’s eye, he reached two fingers into his coat pocket and drew out a single card: ?

‘We’re with some new friends,’ Inji explained. ‘Skinker drugged us. Put poison in the stew. Then he loaded us into a crate and sold us to someone dodgy.

This bloke is called Pyewacket. Him and his lady friend saved us.'

Pyewacket peered over his shoulder, giving them all a tusky smile. 'Morning, chaps! You're just in time. I'm frying up some breakfast. The baker's boy has been, the coffee's on the stove, and all is right with the world.'

'Bacon?' A droplet of dribble escaped the side of Sil's mouth. They usually only had stale bread for breakfast. A bit of five-day-old porridge if they were lucky.

'Sharp as a tack, that one, isn't he?' Pyewacket said. 'What's he called?'

'He's Sil. Short for Silas. I'm Inji. And this is Glyph.'

'Unusual names,' said Pyewacket. He took the skillet off the stove and started spooning bacon on to some plates that had been laid out on the kitchen table. A pile of fresh bread rolls was stacked there as well. Inji's stomach gurgled loudly at the sight of it all.

'They're Romany,' Inji explained. 'Well, Sil's and mine are. Glyph is just called that because of his cards.'

'Cards?' Pyewacket pulled out a chair and sat at

the table. He motioned for them to do the same, and they almost knocked each other over, desperate to get there first.

'He doesn't speak,' said Inji, trying to shove hot bacon into her mouth and snatch a bread roll at the same time. 'He just flips his cards over. They always come out with the words he wants to say. Or numbers. He can guess any number you think of. Or any combination for a safe. That's why Skinker kept him.'

'That's a good trick,' said Pyewacket. 'I have many talents myself, you know. I am currently about to become a businessman. You may have noticed my unique product last night. Or smelt it, at least.'

'Do you mean those disgusting poo-balls you were throwing?' Inji wrinkled her nose at the thought.

'The very same!' Pyewacket grinned, looking smug. 'A stink-based defence system is what I'm calling it. Keeps muggers and thieves at a safe distance. Every person in London will want them, you mark my words! I just need to perfect the recipe and then I can go into production. Would you like a free sample?'

Inji and Glyph both shook their heads. They couldn't imagine anything they would like less. Sil, however, was too focused on the bacon to even notice Pyewacket existed.

'What're your life stories, then?' Pyewacket asked. 'Parents? Families?'

Inji swallowed the last piece of one roll and reached for another. They were so *fresh*, so *soft*. 'Our ma died in the workhouse. She was a Romany gypsy. We think Glyph's mother died on the street. She worked in a big house, he says. It's difficult to get much out of him.'

'More sob stories!' Pyewacket chortled. 'I was sold off for tuppence and a bottle of ale. Sheba's mum ran off from India with her, but died on the boat. We're a houseful of snot-nosed orphans!'

'Speak for yourself, Pyewacket. My nose is delightfully clean at all times.' Sheba had silently entered the room and was now standing by the table. She looked so different to the night before. Rather than the torn shirt and trousers, she was wearing a long skirt, black with white flowers, and a white silk shirt with an ornate silver brooch at her neck. Her waist was cinched tight with a wide bow of orange ribbon, from which a matching silk purse hung. Her hair was piled up in a fashionable bun, held in place by two metal combs. She looked very much a lady, making

Inji suddenly ashamed of her rags, her tangled mop of knotted hair and the way they were all cramming food into their mouths like pigs at a trough.

'Ooh, look at me!' Pyewacket put on a high voice and pretended to flounce. 'My nose is so beautiful and perfect. It *never* has any bogeys in it!'

To Inji's surprise, both Sil and Glyph began to laugh. Sil snorted crumbs of bread everywhere, and Glyph opened his mouth wide in silent mirth. She had never known the pair of them relax around new people so quickly.

Ignoring Pyewacket, Sheba took a bread roll and a plate for herself, then began to pour them all coffee. 'When we've finished breakfast,' she said, 'perhaps you would feel like answering some questions?'

Inji bristled. *And then you'll kick us out straight after*, she thought. Although she couldn't blame them. Who would want three extra freakish mouths to feed? They'd had a good night's sleep and a delicious breakfast: that was probably as good as it was going to get. She nodded her head, still chewing, and gave Sheba a sidelong glance, trying to work out how to twist things so they could stay longer.

'Not just yet,' Pyewacket interrupted her plotting.

'We have to give them the grand tour first. And I want to see this Glyph chap's party trick. Have we got a safe anywhere, Sheba?'

Sheba pushed her bottom lip out in a pout as she thought. 'I've got a lockbox in the workshop somewhere . . .'

'Perfect!' Pyewacket shouted, running out of the kitchen. Inji heard a door open and the sound of someone very excited running down some stairs. Before she had finished her third bread roll, Pyewacket was back, panting and holding a metal container the size of a toolbox. It was held shut by an ornate padlock, with four numbered dials set in the side. He plonked it on the table in front of Glyph and pointed to it with a flourish.

'Go on, then. Show us yer stuff!'

Glyph, still chewing his way through a bacon roll, looked at Inji first. When she nodded, he reached into the pocket of his threadbare velvet coat and brought out his deck of cards.

Thick, mismatched, dog-eared and crumpled as they were, he still managed to shuffle them with uncanny speed. Some were old playing cards, some scavenged bits of pasteboard. Scraps of packets, flaps of boxes; Glyph had gathered them over the years, painstakingly selecting them according to his own secret needs. Each one was marked with a letter or number in spidery black Indian ink.

They slipped and slid over each other, flipping and flapping in a dance. Glyph added a few flourishes, twisting cards over and around his nimble fingers and making Pyewacket coo.

This went on for several minutes, Glyph's pink tongue poking from the corner of his mouth in concentration. Finally, apparently satisfied, he held the deck over the table and thwipped down four cards, one after the other. *Fnap, fnap, fnap, fnap!*

'Four, seven, five, two,' read Pyewacket. 'Go on, Sheba. Try it out.'

Sheba's wide eyes showed that she already knew the combination was correct, but she turned the dials round anyway. There was a *click* as the padlock popped open.

'By the Duke of Wellington's wellingtons!' said Pyewacket.

'That's amazing,' Sheba agreed. She gave Glyph a broad smile, and the boy practically melted. *I wonder if he noticed her* teeth, Inji thought, surprised at the twinge of jealousy she felt. The cat's claws prickled at the tips of her fingers. *Hush*, she told it. *I'm going to learn how to meditate you away, you know.*

Pyewacket was up out of his seat again, snatching everyone's plates and almost throwing them into the wide china sink in the corner. 'Well,' he said, 'seeing as you're our first proper house guests, I suppose I should give you a tour.'

Glyph and Sil hopped down from their seats, clearly excited to explore somewhere new. Pyewacket was beaming at the chance to show off to an audience. It was like watching a bunch of schoolchildren at play, and Inji got a glimpse of how lonely it must be, just Pyewacket and Sheba in this big, empty house together. *Maybe they'll let us stay after all.* Whatever happened, she was going to get at least another day's food and board out of this if she could, because then – she knew – they would be out on the streets.

Cold, harsh, dangerous. Even on her own she would struggle to survive, but with Sil and Glyph to care for as well . . . it didn't bear thinking about.

'Where are you taking them first?' Sheba asked, rising from her chair as well. She gave Inji an exasperated look, as if dealing with Pyewacket was a chore that never ended.

'To the workshop, of course! The site where I created my miraculous invention! Come on!'

Pyewacket led them out of the kitchen, into the hall. He paused beside the staircase and waited for them to assemble before gesturing like a tour guide.

'Upstairs you have the bedrooms – quite boring – and, of course, the water closet.'

'Water closet?' Inji had never heard of such a thing.

'A bog, you idiot,' said Pyewacket, rolling his huge eyes. 'A toilet, a crapper, a throne, a porcelain plop-gobbler. An *indoor* one too, with a chain what you pull so that your doings are flushed out into the Thames.'[v]

There was a gasp from everyone except Sheba, who was hiding her face behind her hand.

'Pyewacket! Do you have to?' Sheba's delicate cheeks were red with fury or embarrassment. Inji couldn't tell which. Sil and Glyph were trying to hide their sniggers.

'Anyway,' said Pyewacket, ignoring her. 'Feast your peepers on *this*.'

He put one hand against the wood panelling of the staircase and pushed. There was a *click*, and a section swung open, revealing a set of stone steps leading downwards. 'Secret stairway!' Pyewacket grinned. 'How amazing is *that*?'

He headed down the stairs, long arms swinging so low they brushed the steps. Sheba motioned for everyone else to follow.

It went against every survival instinct in Inji's body: going down into the cellar of a house with some people she didn't really know. Her mind raced, trying to think of a polite way to refuse, but Sil had already started down the steps, with Glyph following. She had no choice but to go too, although she allowed her inner cat to tweak its claws. They pressed against the skin of her fingertips, ready to pop free if she needed them.

Sil and Glyph clearly trusted these people. And she wanted to as well, but … cellars? Darkness. Traps. She'd read enough lurid newspaper articles about murders to be worried.

Not that she needed to be. Instead of dinginess, damp and mould, they stepped out into a clean, well-lit room with freshly painted walls. The ceiling was quite high, supported by arches, with shelf-filled alcoves all around. It smelt of sawdust, oil and paint. More like a workshop than a cellar.

As if to emphasise that, there were two big workbenches along the side wall, packed with tools and pieces of half-finished projects. And there were more things stacked on the shelves or hanging from hooks. Inji took a closer look, and let out a low whistle.

The first thing she saw was a pistol, a wind-up one, in a display case with lots of miniature feathered darts. Then there was a lady's parasol, all creamy lace and frills, except there was a trigger in the handle and a narrow slot to load bullets in. The pointed end had a hole too. One that looked like a gun barrel.

Inji's eyes flicked from object to object, growing wider with each marvel. A set of telescopic goggles. A corset with armour plating. A powder compact with a handwritten sign next to it, saying: *Danger: deadly poison.*

'What ... what is all this stuff?' she managed to say.

'Tools of the trade,' said Sheba. 'All things we use when we're helping a client. I like to tinker down here. Inventing this and that. Don't touch that, dear.' She gently took a perfume bottle away from Glyph, which had a luggage label on it saying: *Highly explosive.*

'And over *here*,' said Pyewacket, pointing to a

battered chemistry set, 'is where I created the first poo-ball. I expect they'll put it in a museum one day, when my business has become world-famous.'

Inji was amazed. 'You two? You made all of *this*?'

'Well, I only come down here to perfect Pyewacket's Putrid Poo Projectiles every now and then,' said Pyewacket. 'It's Sheba's place, really. Although she did have a bit of help setting it up from her gentleman friend.' He gave Sheba a wink.

'He is *not* my "gentleman friend",' said Sheba, scowling. 'And I'll thank you to stop calling him that. He is a generous relation. That's all.'

'Is he the one who got you this house?' Inji asked, remembering their conversation from last night.

'In a way,' said Sheba. 'The house was my parents' and should have been mine. But when my mother and I disappeared from society, they all thought me dead. The gentleman in question – his name is Lucas Garrow – found out I was alive, and then he made sure I received my inheritance. He also helped me buy all this equipment and taught me how to use it. He shares a passion for . . . inventing.'

'That's not all he shares a passion for,' said Pyewacket, nudging Glyph and smirking. 'And he's only a distant cousin, which means there'll be nothing in the way of you two getting married … except for his evil father.'

'Evil father?' Inji's pointed ears pricked up.

'Yes,' said Pyewacket, rubbing his hands together as he unfolded the tale. '*Lord* Garrow, no less. One of the richest men in England! But as well as practically being royalty, he *hates* anyone like us. He can't stand the fact that Sheba is related to him, and especially that she and his son like to stare into each other's eyes and whisper sweet nothings …'

'That's *enough*!' Sheba shouted at Pyewacket, making almost everyone in the room jump. Not Inji, though. She'd been staring at Sheba when she lost her cool and had got a glimpse of her true side. Only for a split second, but enough to see the wolf. Her teeth had flashed, her eyes had blazed and the shape of her nose had changed. Just a hint of a muzzle, pushing through.

Inji knew, if she'd let it, the change would have overtaken Sheba. There'd have been fur and claws and fangs and snarling.

Instead of scaring Inji, these things made the first glimmer of trust begin to grow in her. *We know,* she told the cat in her head. *We know just what* that *feels like.*

After the outburst, there was an awkward silence. Pyewacket sulked. Sheba blushed. The two boys just stared. Inji realised it was up to her to change the subject.

'Where does that go, over there?' she said, pointing to an ancient-looking iron-banded door in the corner.

'Oooh!' Pyewacket skipped over to it, his sulk forgotten. 'Behind it, there's a secret tunnel. Goes all the way down to the river. *And* an underground chamber, with a broken crab machine in it. Huge great thing it is. We discovered it on our first ever adventure, back when we were nippers. I'll take you down and show you, if you like. You'll have to watch out for rats and eels, mind.'

Sil and Glyph clung to each other, their faces terrified. Everyone else laughed.

'Pyewacket, don't tease them,' said Sheba. 'Come, let's go back upstairs and have some tea. We need to talk about last night, so we may pursue our investigation.'

Here it comes, thought Inji. *And when they've got*

what they want, we'll all be out the door.

But she couldn't blame Sheba. It didn't matter how similar they were; Sil, Glyph and herself were burdens, whatever way you looked at it. *We would have made good investigators, though*, she thought regretfully. *You could have said we were born for it.*

With feet heavy on the stairs, she followed her hosts back up to the parlour.

*

While Sheba and Pyewacket were in the kitchen, making tea, Inji took the chance to whisper to the others.

'Oi, you two! Listen close . . . let me do the talking. I mean, I know neither of you really *talks*, but . . . let me handle this. We've got to get as much out of these coves as we can, because very soon we'll be out on the streets.'

Sil was transfixed by a framed map of Old London on the wall, tracing the streets with a stubby finger, and wasn't even looking at her. Glyph raised his eyebrows and put out his lip.

'I know, I know,' whispered Inji. 'They've been

nice to us. But we've got nowhere to go. We can't go back to Skinker's – unless it's to scratch his evil eyes out – and I'm not having us join another sideshow, not for all nine of my lives. But I don't want us to starve, either . . .'

She was interrupted by footsteps on the corridor, and quickly sat herself in an armchair, just as Pyewacket walked in, carrying a tray with tea things on. Sheba followed and sat down herself.

'Right,' said Pyewacket. 'Who wants tea? And there's some macaroons as well, fresh from the baker's.'

Inji cleared her throat. She looked at the floor, hating herself for the words she was about to say, but knowing they had to be said.

'Before you start, I think we need to agree on a price. I don't mean to be rude, and we're not ungrateful – you saved our lives, after all, and gave us food and everything – but once you're done with us and we leave here, we've got nowhere to go. We've all been on the streets before, and we know how hard it is. We don't like to ask, but we can't expect . . .'

'Wait.' Sheba held up a hand, cutting her off in mid-flow. 'You misunderstand, Inji.'

'Yes,' added Pyewacket. 'What makes you think we're going to throw you out?'

Inji frowned at both of them. 'You're . . . you're not?'

'Of course not,' said Sheba. 'You're all welcome to stay here while we bring down the Hunters' Club.'

'What's ours is yours,' said Pyewacket. 'Although be careful with the toilet, Sil. I don't want your bony bottom cracking my lovely porcelain.'

'And once it's done,' Sheba continued, 'we won't expect you to leave until you've got somewhere safe to go.'

'Really?' Inji could hardly speak. Glyph was beaming and hugging Sil tight.

'We've both had hard times,' said Pyewacket. 'We know how tough it is. You should have seen the trash heap we lived in before.'

'I . . . I don't know what to say . . .' Inji blushed underneath her fur, so ashamed that she had been about to demand money from these kind people.

'You don't have to say anything,' said Sheba. 'Any information you can give us about the Hunters' Club will be thanks enough.'

'Of course! Ask away!' Now the threat of the streets had gone, Inji felt herself relax. At least for a heartbeat. Then the full memory of last night came flooding back in. *Skinker had sold them to their deaths! The Hunters' Club had nearly snatched them!* She found she wanted to catch them every bit as much as Sheba. Catch them and show them why it was never a good idea to upset a wildcat.

'Did you see the man who took you? Would you be able to describe him to us at all?'

Inji shook her head. 'I woke up in the crate. I could only see through a small knothole. He was tall, dressed in leather. He had a mask. Some kind of animal . . . a fox, I think . . .'

Sheba frowned. 'Shame you didn't get a better look. Could you tell us anything else about him? His scent, maybe?'

'I know she's furry, but she might not be able to sniff things out like you,' said Pyewacket.

It was true. Inji's sense of smell was good, but not wolflike. 'I did hear his voice,' she remembered. 'He sounded proper posh. Like a toff.'

'That's a start,' said Sheba. 'And what about the days leading up to the snatch? Was there anyone unusual at the house? Did Mr Skinker have any visitors?'

Inji thought hard, but nothing came to mind. 'Me and Sil were out most of every day. Doing jobs.' *But Glyph wasn't*, she suddenly thought. *He never left the place. Just sat in the kitchen, playing with his cards.*

She turned to her friend, crouching a little to look him in the eyes.

'Glyph,' she said. 'You were at the house. Did anyone come to see Skinker? Anyone new? Not one of his gang . . . someone posh? Well-spoken?'

Everyone stared at Glyph, holding their breath. Finally, he nodded his head, holding up one finger.

'One person!' Inji pointed to his coat pocket, where he kept his cards. 'Can you describe him for us? Can you spell it out?'

Glyph nodded again. He took his battered pack of cards out and sat cross-legged on the parlour floor. After riffling the cards through a few times, he began to deal them out from the top.

Fnap, fnap, fnap . . .

Seven cards, face down. With everyone staring intently, he began to turn them over.

R-E-D-T-A-S-H

'Redtash? What's that?' said Pyewacket. 'His cards have gone wrong!'

Inji groaned. Of all the times for Glyph to lose his gift, it had to be now, didn't it? She reached out, about to snatch the nonsense cards from the floor, when Sheba cried out.

'Stop! Don't touch them! I think I know what it means!'

Chapter Five

In which Mr Skinker meets a grisly end.

They were all bunched around Glyph on the parlour floor, staring down at the cards he had dealt.

'*Redtash*,' said Sheba. 'It's two words: RED and TASH. Glyph, did the man you saw have a moustache? Was it ginger? An orangey-red colour?'

Glyph nodded.

'I take it back,' said Pyewacket. 'The kid's a genius. Let's get him to tell us the combination of the safe with the Crown Jewels in. Or the way into the vaults of the Bank of England.'

'Did you get a good look at him?' Sheba asked,

ignoring Pyewacket. 'Would you be able to draw or describe him for us?'

Glyph made a seesaw motion with his hands. He held up his finger and thumb, a quarter of an inch apart.

'He was too far away,' Inji translated. 'He didn't see him very well.'

Sheba knelt down, so she could look into Glyph's eyes. 'What about his voice? Did you hear him speak?'

Glyph nodded. He reached for his cards again and snapped four on to the parlour rug as quick as a blink.

T-O-F-F

'A toff!' Inji flexed her claws. 'He must have been the one who took us last night!'

'I'm afraid there's more than one gent who speaks like that in London,' said Pyewacket. 'There's a positive plague of 'em. Mr Redtash could've been anybody.'

Inji shook her head. 'Not at Skinker's. Nobody like that ever came there. His crooked friends were all common as muck. Most of them couldn't even string three words together to make a sentence, let alone talk like there was a plum in their mouth.'

'There's a good chance,' said Sheba, 'that Inji is right. I think Glyph may be our first witness to have actually seen a member of the Hunters' Club without a mask. Him and your delightful Mr Skinker, of course.'

Inji nodded. Then a thought occurred to her. 'You're going to want to speak to him, aren't you?'

'Skinker?' said Sheba, standing up and brushing the creases from her skirt. 'Why, yes. But don't worry – Pyewacket and I can go alone if you tell us the address. You won't have to see him again.'

'Oh, I want to see him all right,' said Inji. The thought of Skinker made the cat in her head bristle and hiss. She remembered seeing a mother cat once, protecting its kittens from a stray dog. It was like a ball of puffed-out fur, deadly claws and boiling fury. And now one was trapped in her head, battering to come out.

'We don't owe him nothing, now. We don't work for him, we don't take orders from him . . . Now he's just a cove who sold me, my brother and my best friend off to be killed. I'm going to go full cat on him, right in his ugly face.'

Glyph gulped, and Sil let out a frightened mew. Even Pyewacket took one look at the rage bubbling behind Inji's eyes and stepped quickly backwards.

But it didn't scare Sheba. She placed her hands on Inji's shoulders and looked within, staring down the snarling wildcat until it wanted to cower and hide.

'Inji. Listen to me. *You* are the one in control. Not the cat. *You* have the right to be angry. To be furious, even. But it's *your* anger – human anger – not an animal one. This Skinker will pay for what he's done, I promise you. And we'll make sure he never does it to another child. But it won't be done with violence and fury. Cold, calm revenge is what we need. We are human beings, not beasts.'

'I would've said you're a bit of both,' said Pyewacket, as quietly as he could. Sheba shot him a look with eyes that flashed amber.

Inji felt Sheba's firm grip. She could see her blazing eyes, see the wolf there too, just behind her gaze, present, but in check.

Breathe, she told herself. *Just breathe.*

Staring at Sheba, breathing slowly, she felt the cat begin to fade. The fur on her body flattened, her claws slid slowly into their sheaths. She was in charge once more – for now at least.

'Jolly good,' said Pyewacket. 'Because we do actually need to chat to this Skinker cove. We can't do that if his face is in ribbons. No matter how much he deserves it.'

Inji allowed herself a smirk, and followed everyone out to the yard. But even as the carriage was made ready, even as they clip-clopped their way through the London streets, even as they crossed the river into the smoky stink of Whitechapel, she could feel the tips of her razor claws, pushing against the skin of her fingertips, eager to pop free.

*

The carriage pulled up in Church Street, in front of the familiar townhouse with its thick coating of grime. Inji felt the usual twinge of horror at seeing the place, but this time it was combined with several other feelings: a primal mix of rage and hatred for Skinker and also a touch of fear. What would his reaction be when he saw them? Would there be violence? Would they have to chase him?

I hope so, thought the cat, those claws prickling

again. *Shush*, Inji told it. *Bad kitty.*

'I think it best that I knock,' said Sheba, seeing that Inji was about to step up and tap out the secret signal with her knuckles. 'You three are supposed to be tied up in a Hunters' Club dungeon somewhere, remember?'

'Oh yes.' Inji blushed. 'Of course.' She stepped back, cursing her thoughtlessness, ushering Sil and Glyph to the side of the porch, where they wouldn't be seen.

Sheba stepped up to the door and swung the knocker briskly. *Tap, tap tap!* Inji noticed she kept her other hand inside a fur hand-warmer. Was that to keep off the autumn chill, or was it to disguise what she was holding? A pistol, perhaps? One of her outlandish inventions?

There was no answer, not even after three more tries.

'He doesn't appear to be in,' said Sheba. 'Is that normal?'

'No,' said Inji. 'He never goes out, on account of people staring at his face. Everyone always comes here to do business with him.'

'I can climb up and see if a window's open,'

Pyewacket suggested. He was hopping from side to side as if eager to get off the ground.

'You might have to,' said Inji. 'That door has the strongest deadbolt in London.'

'Wait a moment,' said Sheba. She reached into a silk pouch at her waist and brought out a fountain pen. When she popped open the lid, Inji saw a whole array of lockpicks inside; just the sort of thing a burglar might carry.

'Hold this, please.' She passed her fur hand-warmer to Pyewacket, giving Inji a glimpse of the pistol handle inside. Then she pulled out two lockpicks and set to work on the door. A few seconds later, there was a *clunk* and it swung open.

'Blimey,' said Inji, impressed. 'If Skinker saw that, he'd probably give you a job.'

Sheba smiled. 'Just a little talent I picked up when I was a girl,' she said. 'In we go.'

I'll ask you about it later, Inji thought. She set an arm around Glyph and Sil, and stepped back into their old home.

*

'Mr Skinker? Mr Skinker? Hello?'

No answer to Sheba's calls. The house was silent. A heavy, ominous, *wrong* silence. Inji felt the hair on her neck prickle.

But nothing *seemed* different. The same bare floorboards, same staircase, same corridor leading down to the kitchen.

They went there first, feet creaking the floorboards.

'Is this where you slept?' Sheba asked, noticing the pile of filthy hessian sacks.

'This is where we did everything,' said Inji. 'We weren't allowed anywhere else in the house.'

The room was just the same as they had left it. Inji's bowl of half-eaten stew still sat on the table, now covered in a thick coating of cold grease.

'Bed?' said Sil, shuffling over to the sacks.

'Not now, Sil,' said Inji. 'We're not staying. Just visiting Skinker, that's all.'

'Skinker,' Sil repeated. He looked nervous, like he wanted to be somewhere else. Back in the nice house with the bacon and tea. Inji knew how he felt.

'This Skinker,' said Pyewacket. 'Lives upstairs, does he?'

Inji nodded. Sheba was scanning the room, taking in every detail. Then she lifted her head and began to sniff, her delicate nostrils flaring.

'I can pick up a trace of someone upstairs,' she said. 'And there's blood.'

Inji flinched at the word. She tried sniffing herself, but all she could make out was the usual stink of the house: greasy stew, old boots, coal dust, gas lamps, damp ... although there was a chill atmosphere about the place that had never been there before. An evil kind of cold that made her fur bristle.

Death, said her cat senses. *Somebody has died here.*

'Let's go up, then,' said Sheba. She nodded to Pyewacket, who slid a catapult from his back pocket and fitted one of his Putrid Poo Projectiles to it.

They walked back to the foot of the staircase and looked upwards. It was dingy, choked full of shadows – no lamps lit or curtains drawn. Inji imagined pools of blood trickling down the stairs. She found her feet wouldn't move when she tried to go up the first step. Behind her, Sil and Glyph were both crying.

'What's the matter?' Sheba asked.

'We . . . we're not allowed upstairs,' Inji said. The lesson had been literally beaten into them with boots and sticks and fists. 'Skinker doesn't like it.'

'Skinker isn't in charge of you any more,' said Sheba. 'You don't have to be afraid of him.'

'I'm not,' Inji said quickly, knowing it was a lie. 'But Sil and Glyph are. Maybe they could stay here?'

'Good thinking,' said Sheba. 'Pyewacket, you stay with them.'

'Do what?' said Pyewacket. 'I'm a businessman, not a babysitter, you know.'

But he stayed where he was and, at a nod from Sheba, began to talk to the boys in a quiet, soothing voice. Once their whimpering had stopped, Sheba started up the stairs. Inji swallowed back her jitters and followed after.

*

It seemed very strange to be standing on the first-floor landing, after all those months of wondering what was up there. The walls and floorboards were bare, just like downstairs. There were two doors in front of them, another further down the corridor, and everything was dark. That didn't bother Inji or Sheba, though – they could both see better in the gloom than most people could in broad daylight.

'I think the blood's upstairs,' Sheba said. 'But we should probably check these rooms first.'

With Sheba leading, they nudged the doors open and peered inside. Each room was large, with a high ceiling, and was stacked full of *stuff.* There were piles of paintings, statues, lockboxes, crates and suitcases. Silk dresses and handkerchiefs spilled in mounds everywhere. Boxes of silver cutlery, pearls, lockets, wallets and candlesticks lined the walls. It was like a secret grotto, a cave of stolen wonders from a fairy tale.

Inji blinked, her mouth hanging open. 'He … he had all *this*? All these things? And we were downstairs, half starved and sleeping on rags?'

'Your Mr Skinker was quite the fence,'[vi] said Sheba. 'He must have had all the gangs in the East End thieving for him.'

'And us as well,' said Inji, her voice quiet. Seeing all those piles of goods, all those treasures that must have been loved and missed by their owners … she felt a sudden, deep pang of guilt at what she had been a part of.

'It wasn't your fault.' Sheba seemed to know just what she was feeling. 'You had no choice. You were just surviving – doing what you had to. If you have to be angry at someone, make it Skinker.'

Inji nodded, not trusting her voice at that moment. She *was* angry with Skinker all right – a whole ton of angries, piled on top of each other – except she had a bad feeling they were going to find him somewhere on the next floor. And when they did, it wouldn't be pretty. What use was her anger if there was nobody alive to vent it on?

Head swimming with emotions she didn't really understand, she followed Sheba up the final staircase.

*

There was a single room at the top. A big one that filled the entire floor. Its door stood half open, smoky darkness seeping out. Inji could smell the blood now. A coppery, meaty scent that made her stomach lurch. It reminded her of sick people at the workhouse:

dying wretches, coughing their lungs up into buckets and scraps of rags.

'Mr Skinker?' Sheba called. Her voice was swallowed by the blackness welling through the door crack. She drew the pistol from her fur hand-warmer and pulled the hammer back with a tiny *click.*

Step by step, almost tiptoeing, they made their way forward, until Sheba could touch the wood of the door. She pushed it, making it swing inwards with a long, slow *creeeeak.*

'Mr Skinker?' she said again.

Inji had seen lots of dead bodies in her time. Mostly in the workhouse, but also a few on the streets. Once there had been a carriage accident: a young woman had been trampled by the horses and killed in an instant.

Those poor folk had always looked peaceful after dying. Like they were asleep, and their troubles finally over.

Tannikin Skinker didn't.

He was sitting in a high-backed leather armchair, facing the door. His hands were in his lap, fingers grasping. His ugly face was thrown back, clearly showing the hole in his cheek. His pale, stained skin was white and waxy, his mouth twisted in shock or fright, and the front of his stained smoking jacket was black with clotted blood.

But the worst thing was his eyes. They were wide and terrified, staring out at Inji as if he could still see her. She stifled a sob and looked away quick. The man was a monster, but even so … to end up like that …

'Why don't you look around the room?' Sheba suggested. 'I will examine the body. Or you could go back downstairs, if it would make you feel better. There's no danger here.'

'I … I'll stay,' said Inji. She wanted to prove herself somehow. She wanted to be like Sheba, who hadn't even flinched when she saw what was left of Skinker.

'Very good,' Sheba said. She unpinned the silver brooch from her neck and pressed the centre. The hidden lens of a magnifying glass popped out. 'Let's get to work,' she said.

Inji nodded, and turned away from the armchair with its hideous contents. She focused her attention on the room itself.

And what a room it was! Even in the darkness,

it looked grand. The throne room of a hidden robber-king, living in luxury while his servants starved below.

There were several thick, beautifully patterned rugs on the floor, soft and squishy under Inji's feet. Wide windows filled the right-hand wall, covered over now by heavy velvet curtains. Behind them, Inji imagined she would have a view of the townhouses across the street, and behind that the white spire of Hawksmoor's church, rising up into the sky.

But the curtains are still drawn, she thought. *That means he must have been killed in the night. He wasn't alive to open them come the morning.*

The walls had patterned wallpaper and were fitted with beautiful glass gas lamps. There was an ornate mahogany wardrobe, a set of drawers, a chaise longue, more armchairs . . . all of it the best, most expensive furniture. All of it stolen from wealthy houses around London, she expected.

But the most interesting thing was sitting on the desk to the left, opposite the window. An enormous leather-bound journal, its pages pasted full of handbills, scraps of paper, magazine cuttings and fragments of city maps, every page scrawled over with splodges of inky, spidery writing.

Inji moved closer, peering at the masses of evidence. She turned the creaking pages, stiff as boards with layers of yellowing glue. She squinted as she deciphered the spattery scribbles of Skinker's hand.

There were notes about certain houses, shops and offices. Each page had maps, lists of opening times, scrawled notes about who lived there, how they came and went. Paintings and pieces of valuable furniture and jewellery were described or sketched.

This is how he planned his burglaries, Inji realised. *He collected all the information, then sent his goons out to rob these places.*

It was very well organised, she had to give Skinker credit.

Inji turned to the last full page, finding a drawing of the place in Lambeth they had robbed yesterday. Pasted beneath was a scribbled confession about where the photographs were hidden; a list of the Lads themselves; even a detailed pencil map of their base and the surrounding roads.

Use the twins, was scrawled in the margin, in Skinker's messy writing.

She looked for any mention of a deal with the Hunters' Club. A name, a meeting place. How much that rat had sold them out for.

Nothing. Whatever had passed between them, Skinker had thought it best not to keep a record.

'Found anything?' Sheba asked.

Inji risked a glance across and saw Sheba examining Skinker's wound with the magnifying glass. Her stomach lurched and she quickly looked away again.

'This book was where he planned everything,' she said. 'Every job he ever organised, I reckon. The peelers would love to see this.'

'We shall inform them once we have left,' said Sheba. 'Perhaps they can return some of the stolen valuables.'

'I hope so,' said Inji. She felt a pang of guilt again, at having been a part of all this in whatever way. She should have just taken the boys and run away. She should have refused to steal for the horrid ogre.

'Did he have any enemies?' Sheba asked, still peering at Skinker. 'Anyone who might have done this?'

'Take your pick,' said Inji. Skinker was always

stealing from other gangs; treading on toes, playing people off against each other. She thought about the Lambeth Lads. The last thing they'd shouted was about getting Skinker back. 'Half the gangs in London wanted to kill him.'

'This was no gang killing,' said Sheba. 'The place would have been ransacked. There's hundreds of pounds' worth of silver here, all untouched.'

'Someone rich, then?' said Inji. 'Someone who wouldn't want his money?'

'Yes,' said Sheba. 'And someone he knew. He let them in without a struggle. They came up here, and then Skinker was dispatched. Quickly and quietly. Very professional.'

'It happened at night,' said Inji. 'The curtains are still drawn.'

'Very good,' said Sheba. 'Yes. From the state of the body, I'd say it was two or three o'clock in the morning. Right about when we were heading for bed.'

'Do you think it was them?' Inji asked. 'The Hunters' Club, I mean?'

Sheba was now looking at Skinker's hands, bent over them with her magnifying glass. 'I would guess so,' she said. 'They would have been furious that you escaped. And they would have known Skinker was a witness. He would have had to be silenced, in case you went to the police . . . Aha!'

Having spotted a clue with her glass, Sheba quickly fished a pair of silver tweezers from the purse at her belt. She bent down again, plucking something from one of Skinker's fingernails.

'Inji,' she said. 'The curtains, please.'

Inji darted over to the window and pulled back one of the drapes, letting in a burst of smoky autumn sunshine. The sudden change in light made her blink.

'I thought so,' said Sheba, holding her tweezers up and gazing through her glass. 'Come and see.'

Not wanting to get too near to the body, Inji edged closer, peering through the glass that Sheba held out. Clutched in the tweezers was a hair, one that Skinker must have grabbed when he was fighting with his attacker.

It was a very dark shade of ginger. Almost red.

'Redtash,' Inji whispered.

'Indeed,' said Sheba. 'Our hunter must have returned here after your rescue. We know who killed your old boss, but now the trail has gone cold. The one person who could have identified him is dead.'

Sheba dropped the hair to the floor and slid the tweezers back in her purse. She walked over to the book and began to flick through it, frowning. Inji could sense her frustration … to come so close to getting an answer, and now nothing …

Inji peered over Sheba's shoulder at the turning pages. Could there be anything there? Some other clue? Another witness? Her eyes caught on an old playbill, half hidden by a clutch of notes and sketches. She snatched it out and held it up to read.

'This Redtash,' she said. 'We know he's a posh gent, right?'

'We believe so,' said Sheba. 'If his accent is anything to go by.'

'But how would someone like that find out about me and the boys? Skinker kept us a secret, mostly. The other gangs in the underworld knew about us, but none of them would peach to an outsider. There's a code between them all, you know.'

'What are you getting at?' Sheba asked, turning her attention from the book to Inji.

'Redtash would have had to know Skinker had some sideshow acts in his keeping. But he couldn't have just strolled up and asked about us in a pub.

Nobody from the East End would let slip a fact like that. Not to some cove with a plum in his mouth.'

'So he'd have had to find out from someone else!'

'Exactly.' Inji held up the playbill for Sheba to see. *Madam Pasternak's Circus of the Bizarre*, it read. *Come and be horrified. Sick buckets supplied.*

'Old Redtash must have been asking around for sideshow acts to capture and hunt. Where else would he have gone, except to the showmasters? And the only one who knew where Sil and I were sold off to was Madam Pasternak. Our last owner before Skinker.'

'Inji,' said Sheba, gently taking the playbill from her fingers. 'You are a very clever girl. And you might just have found us a new witness. Let's go and tell the others the news.'

As Inji followed Sheba down the stairs, she couldn't help puffing out her chest with pride. In her head, the cat rolled over on to its back and purred.

Very clever girl, she thought, repeating the words over and over to herself. It was, she realised, the only nice thing anyone had ever said to her. It even made her forget about the body of Skinker, frozen in its horrible pose.

From the leather armchair, the cold, dead eyes of her old boss watched as she left his house of thievery for good.

Chapter Six

In which our heroes are reunited with a cruel villain.

Madam Pasternak's Circus of the Bizarre. Just one in a long string of sideshows they had been owned by.

Their stay had been a short but unpleasant one, Inji remembered.

The home of the Circus was little more than a back room in a crumbling old Cheapside pub called the Three Castles. The acts were few, and dodgy at best. There had been her and Sil; Elspeth Merrywhisker the bearded lady; Benjamin Bendylegs the contortionist and Gobbleguts the glutton.

They did a piece every night, just before closing

time, playing to a room full of screaming punters, half crazy with gin. Having bottles and glasses hurled at you was part of the job.

First on was always Elspeth. She danced about in a dress, stroking her beard and singing a few rude songs. Not that you could hear anything she sang over all the insults being yelled at her.

Benjamin was usually up next. His act was mainly getting himself in and out of a small tea chest by bending his limbs in all sorts of strange ways. On one particularly rowdy night, an audience member had set the chest on fire with him in it. Inji had had to throw a pitcher of beer over him to put it out.

Then it was her and Sil's turn. She basically just hissed and scratched a lot. Sometimes she climbed up the walls with her claws. Sil had to stand there, his back turned, while Madam Pasternak asked the crowd to throw bottles and bricks at him. Inji knew that Sil's bone plates would protect him, but it was still horrible to watch. Except for the times one of the yobs would get hit with his own brick as it bounced back. That was most satisfying.

Gobbleguts was always the last act. He could eat anything: plates, glasses, rocks, slippery eels from the Thames. She even saw him swallow a dead dog once. And then, as the crowd began to flee in disgust, Madam Pasternak sent out Gruno and Bruno, her two muscle-bound heavies, to clear the room completely. Their favourite pastime was listening to the crackle of broken fingers and noses as they sent everyone packing.

As for Pasternak herself, well, she was nowhere near as exotic as her name sounded. In fact, according to Elspeth, it wasn't her real name at all.

She was a broad, squat beefcake of a woman, with a face like a bulldog gargling vinegar. Her skin was ruddy and blotched, as if she'd been freshly scrubbed with a wire-bristled brush, and her eyes were mean little slits of hate.

There were rumours that she used to be a baby farmer, taking in children whose parents were unable to look after them (for a fee, of course).[vii] Elspeth said that the crushers had come a bit too close to arresting Pasternak after several babies in her care 'disappeared', and that she had set up a sideshow instead. What started out as a disguise turned out to be a good earner. Her acts only needed a bowl of gruel and some filthy water once a day. Just enough to keep them alive. The rest went in her pocket, or on pastries for her two enormous bouncers. Inji remembered actually being relieved when Skinker asked to buy them. How stupid *that* was.

All this ran through her head as they made their way to Cheapside.

They dropped off the horse and carriage at a stable yard on the way, then headed up Lombard Street on foot. Inji wrapped her shawl about her, and Pyewacket tucked his trailing arms deep into his trouser pockets. At first glance, they appeared to be an ordinary family, out for a stroll.

Although what would a posh lady like Sheba be doing with three scruffy urchins? Inji thought. As if reading her mind, Sheba reached over and plucked at her threadbare shawl.

'When we get a chance, we shall have to find you three some decent outfits,' she said.

Inji blinked in surprise. She had never had new clothes before. Everything she wore was made up of patches upon patches. You could barely guess what material it had once been made of. But shopping for a new wardrobe would have to wait.

'We need to survive Madam Pasternak first,' Inji

said. 'She has two heavies, you know. Gruno and Bruno they're called. We used to reckon they were leftovers from her baby-farming days. She's fed them up to the size of hippopotamuses. They're a vicious pair of thugs.'

'Oh,' said Sheba, a slight smile twitching at the corner of her mouth. 'I think you'll find Pyewacket and I can take care of ourselves.'

*

They reached the Three Castles not long after lunch. When Sil saw it, he let out a squeak and tried to hide behind Pyewacket.

'It's all right,' said Inji, taking him by the hand. 'We're only visiting. Just saying hello to old Madam Pasternak.'

'Pasternak,' Sil repeated. His usually calm features wrinkled in a snarl.

'Don't you worry, mate,' said Pyewacket. 'We'll be in and out. A quick chat, then it's back home for some bacon butties.'

'Bacon?' Sil's eyes lit up and he smacked his lips.

'Oh yes,' said Pyewacket. 'And if you're lucky, you

can help me cook up a new batch of Poo Projectiles. I only have a few of these beauties left.'

'Let's concentrate on the matter at hand, shall we?' said Sheba. She pushed open one of the pub's swing doors.

Inside, the place was almost empty, just one or two drunkards snoozing in the corner. It was more of a barn than a pub, with a splintery old bar and a few battered chairs. Your feet stuck to the floorboards as you walked, and the whole place stank of stale beer.

Old Winston, the bartender, was on duty, lazily polishing glasses with the filthiest rag in London. He looked up as they entered and blinked when he saw Sheba.

She must be the finest customer that's ever walked through these doors, Inji thought. Winston blinked again when he recognised Inji and Sil.

''Ello,' he said. 'What're you two blighters doing back 'ere? And why are you with 'er ladyship there?'

'We've come to speak with Madam Pasternak,' said Sheba. Her voice was stern, and she gave Winston an amber-edged glare. 'It's a matter of some importance.'

Winston rubbed at his stained whiskers with the

back of a knobbly hand. He didn't know who it would be worse to offend: Pasternak or this fierce stranger. In the end, he decided the devil he knew was best.

'She's out back,' he said. 'But she doesn't like to be disturbed. I don't want no trouble . . .'

'There will be none, I can assure you,' Sheba said, making for the door to the back room. The others followed her.

'My card.' Pyewacket handed Winston a rectangle of creased paper as he passed. 'I'm developing a range of odour-based defence products, in case you're interested in selling them.'

'It's just an old sweet wrapper with the word "Poo" written on it,' said Winston, bemused.

'Yes, well. I'm developing my business cards as well,' said Pyewacket, with an awkward grin. Then he trotted after Sheba.

Winston gulped and started moving everything breakable somewhere safe.

*

The back room was dark and dingy and, if possible, smelt even worse than the bar. The patchy curtains were drawn across the windows, leaving the corners in deep shadow. A doorway to another room – the cubby where Pasternak and her goons slept – stood ajar. Inji spotted the stage along the far wall, even recognised some of her claw marks still scarring the woodwork. She shuddered.

A chalkboard stood beside the doorway, marked up with a list of acts. Elspeth was still on there, Inji noted, as were Benjamin and Gobbleguts, but their names had been crossed out. There was a blank space where her and Sil's names had once sat. '*Peter Scribbleskin the Tattooed Boy*' had been added over the top.

Down to two acts, Inji thought. *Pasternak has fallen on hard times.*

'Can I 'elp you?' A harsh, growling voice came from the shadows in the corner. Inji instantly knew it as her old owner's.

'I believe you can,' said Sheba. 'We are here to ask you some questions about two of your acts.'

There was a shuffling, and a wide, stumpy figure emerged from the gloom. It was Pasternak, as mean and ugly as ever. There was a strong whiff of stale sweat about her, and her fleshy face was set in a scowl.

'What? Those two?' She jabbed a thumb at Sil and

Inji. 'Never seen 'em before in my life.'

Inji snorted. 'It's *us*, Madam Pasternak. We're standing right in front of you. You can't deny you know us.'

'All right, then,' she said. 'But you can't prove I did nuffink. Didn't touch a hair on them kiddies' heads, I didn't.'

'Actually,' said Sheba, 'we wanted to ask you whether anyone else has been enquiring about them. Perhaps a well-spoken man with a red moustache?'

Pasternak's ruddy face went pale in a heartbeat. She turned her head and bellowed in a voice that would have deafened a sergeant major. 'Gruno! Bruno! Get out here right now! There's some noses that need breaking!'

There was some frantic stomping from the cubby room, and then two hulking men burst out. They looked almost identical to each other, and quite similar to Pasternak herself. Both had bald heads, sloping shoulders and arms like sides of beef. Their noses were flat, their faces scarred and their mouths of broken teeth were set in gleeful grimaces.

'Smashy, smashy!' said one, charging straight at Sheba.

Instead of running, Sheba shifted her posture, turning sideways and sliding into a half-crouch. She spun her arms in a windmill pattern, almost a dance, and stood steady as Gruno (or Bruno) approached.

'Move aside, young 'uns,' said Pyewacket. 'This won't be pretty.' He shepherded them out of the way, back towards the door. Inji strained to see what would happen. She could feel her claws tensing, and that familiar *hiss* building ... She wanted to help Sheba. She wanted to fly at Pasternak herself, raking and spitting.

But Sheba didn't need any help. The first goon reached her, one meaty fist swinging at her delicate nose. As quick as a blink, as graceful as a ballerina, Sheba took hold of his arm and stepped underneath it, turning as she went. Gruno/Bruno carried on moving, his massive bulk sending him shooting over Sheba's back, somersaulting through the air.

Just as he landed, Sheba, still holding his arm, turned around again, giving the limb a sharp twist. There was a *crack*, then a *thump*. The goon's arm broke, a split second before he hit the filthy floorboards with a shockwave that made plaster crumble from the walls.

The other one – Bruno perhaps – roared and began a charge of his own. Sheba calmly reached into the silk sash at her waist and drew out her pistol. She fired it with a *thwip* and a tiny, feathered dart appeared in between Bruno's eyes. He took two more steps, then collapsed like a sack of rotten potatoes.

Madam Pasternak watched all this with her eyes growing wider and wider. Her two precious bullies had just been pasted by a slip of a girl in a posh outfit. But that wasn't the end of it. Sheba was suddenly marching across the room, a look of fury on her face.

She was upon Pasternak in a few steps, her hand flashing out to grab the beefy woman by the right ear. She then twisted the lobe, *hard.*

'Now,' said Sheba. There was the edge of a growl to her voice. 'You *will* tell us what you know. Or the next show you attend will be your funeral.'

'Aaargh!' Pasternak screamed. 'Me ear! Your nails are tearing it!'

Inji moved closer, watching Sheba's face. She was *really* angry. A raw, animal rage. Her nose had jutted forward, almost snoutlike. Her white teeth gleamed, sharp as needles, and her *eyes* ... they were like sparks glimpsed in the darkness between the trees of an ancient forest. The glowing beads of light you saw just before you became dinner.

'Do you know how much I hate sideshow owners?' Sheba snarled the words. 'Do you know what I dream of doing to scum like you?'

'I'll talk! I'll talk!' Pasternak was crying now. There was a sharp, bitter stink in the air, and Inji realised the woman had actually wet herself in terror. 'There was a chap! 'E came 'ere two weeks or so ago! Said 'e was making his own show, somewhere up west. I sold him Bendylegs and Gobbleguts. Then 'e asks if I know of any uvvers. I told him I 'ad some before, but sold 'em on. I wouldn't tell him where at first: Skinker paid me not to. But then 'e gave me anuvver five pound. So I told him Skinker's address. I 'ad to do it! The money . . .'

'Did he have a red moustache?' Sheba twisted Pasternak's ear tighter.

'Owww! Yes! Yes 'e did! And 'e was posh as anyfing!'

'Did he leave a card?' Inji stepped up to join the questioning. She found she was becoming as hungry for answers as Sheba. 'Do you know where to find him?'

‘No!’ Pasternak wailed. ‘There was nuffing! ’E just gave me the money. I don’t know where ’e came from. I never saw him again, I promise!’

‘This is useless!’ Sheba gnashed her teeth. It looked like the wolf was taking control, despite everything she had said to Inji about taming it.

‘Wait!’ Pasternak wailed, pressing her hands together as if she were praying. ‘There is sumfing I can tell you! I know someone you can talk to!’

‘Who?’ said Sheba, giving her ear another tug. ‘Tell me now, and make it good, or you’ll never wear spectacles again!’

‘Gobbleguts!’ Pasternak yelled. ‘A week after I sold him to that posh bloke, ’e came back! Said they took him orf somewhere and hunted him! Spouted a load of nonsense about masks and wolves and foxes. Said ’e got away and it was terrifying. ’E wanted me to hide him, but I told him to jigger off. I’m not getting myself in trouble with gents what hunt down and kill people, not for nobody.’

Sheba began to snarl again, but Inji stepped up. It was her turn to put a hand on Sheba’s shoulder, bringing her back to herself. Sheba blinked, and Inji could see the wolf behind her eyes falter. She had begun to realise what was happening; how she was losing control.

Just before Sheba released Pasternak, Inji jumped in with one last question. 'Where is Gobbleguts now?' she asked. 'Where did he go after leaving you?'

'I'm not sure,' Pasternak said, beginning to sob. 'Don't hurt me, but I'm not sure. I 'eard a rumour that 'e joined the Scarlequins. Just a rumour, but that's all I know. Honest, it is. Please let go of me ear.'

With a gasp, Sheba released the woman. She pulled her hand back and stared at it. Inji got a glimpse of her nails, tweaked into claws. Not as sharp as hers, but enough to do some damage. There was blood on Pasternak's neck where they had pierced the skin.

'My boys, my boys!' Pasternak fell to the floor and scrabbled her way over to where Bruno lay, the dart still jutting from his forehead.

'They'll be fine in a bit,' said Pyewacket. He took Sheba by the arm and began leading her out of the room. 'Well, one of them's probably broken a bone or three, but apart from that . . .'

'Who *are* you people?' Pasternak yelled. '*What* are you?'

Inji bent down to her, smiling her wickedest smile.

'We're the Carnival,' she said. 'And if you haven't told us the truth . . . if we can't find Gobbleguts with these Scarlequins . . . then we'll be *back*.'

They could still hear the woman sobbing as they stepped out of the pub. Loud, honking sobs, like a walrus being murdered. It made Inji smile all the more.

Chapter Seven

In which our heroes are nearly snaffled on their way to the circus.

They stood on the pavement, waiting for Sheba to compose herself. The tide of Londoners flowed around them, like a grimy river breaking over a handful of stubborn rocks.

Normally poised and elegant, she was leaning up against the pub wall, gasping. Tears brimmed in her eyes and every now and then she shook her head hard, as if trying to clear it.

'It's all right, Sheebs,' Pyewacket was saying, over and over. 'You were great in there. You didn't do anything I wouldn't have done.'

'Yes,' Inji agreed. 'You were *amazing.*'

Glyph tugged at Inji's shawl to get her attention. He pointed at Sheba and raised his hands, asking what was wrong. Inji shrugged back at him and shook her head. She had no idea.

Even Sil was concerned. He shuffled up to Sheba, his eyes fixed on the ground, and placed a hand on her arm. Inji was amazed – he never normally noticed when other people were upset.

It was this that brought Sheba back to herself. 'I'm ... so sorry,' she finally managed to say. 'I almost lost control ... I was so angry ...'

'I'm not surprised,' said Inji. 'Two great bruisers just tried to squish you.'

'It wasn't that,' said Sheba. 'It was that woman. The sideshow owner. I can't *stand* sideshow owners.'

Inji remembered the tintype picture on the parlour wall. The one of Sheba and Pyewacket as children, as part of that show. 'Is it because of that Plump-whatshisname? The one who used to own you both?'

Sheba nodded. She took a lace-edged handkerchief from her sash and dabbed at her eyes.

'He was a right horse's backside, and no mistake,'

said Pyewacket. 'Treated us all like dirt, while he lined his pockets.'

'What happened?' Inji asked, before wondering if it was better not to know.

Sheba sighed. 'It was just after my cousin, Mr Garrow, discovered me. I had been secretly visiting my parents' old house, and Mr Garrow had found things I'd left there. Bunches of jasmine under my mother's portrait. Notes I had written to her . . .

'He knew it meant that I was here, in London. His long-lost relative. He waited at Paradise Street for me one day and offered to help me become recognised as my father's heir. And when he found out how I had been living – how badly I had been treated by Plumpscuttle – he was furious. He called the police and reported the brute.'

'And when someone from the upper classes calls the peelers, they jump to it,' said Pyewacket. 'If we'd gone to them ourselves, we'd have been laughed out of the station.'

'What happened to Plumpscuttle?' Inji asked. 'Did he go to prison?'

'Unfortunately not,' Sheba replied. 'When the

police turned up, he ran out the back door and disappeared.'

'He was last seen boarding a steamer, heading for America,' Pyewacket said. 'He must have had some money and a ticket squirrelled away. He's probably in New York right now, tormenting another poor bunch of carnival acts.' He turned and spat on the pavement, making a passing gentleman leap out of the way.

'I apologise again,' said Sheba. 'Those memories are so strong … all my usual techniques for keeping my wolf under control vanished. And after everything I said to you, Inji …'

Inji took Sheba's hand and squeezed it. 'It doesn't matter,' she said. And it didn't. If anything, it made Sheba seem less perfect, more human, more like *her*. 'You got a clue out of Pasternak, don't forget. All we have to do is work out what these Scar-thingies are, and we can find Gobbleguts.'

'Oh,' said Pyewacket, winking. 'The Scarlequins. We know all about *them*, don't we, Sheebs?'

*

Pyewacket filled them in on the details during the walk back to the stable yard.

'We heard about them when we were in the sideshow ourselves,' he said. 'At first we thought it was all nonsense. One of those legends that spring up on the streets, like Spring-heeled Jack or the Cock Lane Ghost.

'But enough people mentioned them for us to be curious. There was talk from other carnival folk we met on the road. Beggars, mudlarks, tinkers and gypsies would mention them. *Had enough of your boss?* they would say. *Run away and join the Scarlequins.*

'Before long, we decided to investigate for ourselves. Didn't take us long to find out they was real. A little longer and we had an invite to one of their performances.'

'Are they a sideshow as well, then?' Inji asked.

'Not really,' Pyewacket continued. 'More of a troupe of their own. It all started, so the story goes, when an Italian carnival was touring London around a hundred years ago. One of the players, some kind of clown, had enough of her boss and legged it. She lived on the streets, doing secret performances for food and money.

'Before long, other runaways left their shows or their masters and joined her. They became a sideshow of their own, but as their own bosses. Free to play wherever they chose. Of course, this wasn't popular with their old owners. They put out rewards and tried to hunt them down, so the Scarlequins had to become even more sneaky.

'They're still going, though, all these years later. Nobody knows where their next performance will be. Word gets out a few days before, and then they appear. Always in hidden places. Secret hideaways and forgotten alleys. And only the people of the streets are invited. Only folk who will appreciate them.'

'But how do they make enough money to eat?' Inji asked. 'Where do they live? Who takes care of them?'

'They charge a fee of whatever folk can spare,' said Pyewacket. 'Food or coin. Trinkets, keepsakes, locks of hair. Secrets and prayers. Some think they manage to live off those scraps in between shows, but I reckon they have a sideline. Burglary, maybe. Pickpocketing. Armed robbery.'

Inji was fascinated. Why hadn't she heard about these runaway showpeople before? 'How is it you know so much about them?' she asked. 'All their history and stuff? Did you get it all from that one visit?'

'Not quite.' Pyewacket gave a sad smile. 'We saw them that time, and then, when Sheba got her inheritance and Plumpscuttle was gone, two of our friends decided to join them. They weren't cut out for life in a posh house, I suppose. Either that, or they had some reason to stay hidden. We never really found out. They just ran off one day and became Scarlequins.'

'Was that the big man?' said Inji. 'And the woman with the rats?'

'Gigantus and Mama Rat.' Sheba had been very quiet all through Pyewacket's speech. She joined in just as they were arriving at the stable. 'They were like parents to us. We miss them so much.'

'But we'll be seeing them again soon, eh?' Pyewacket nudged Sheba and smiled. 'We'll have to go, just to speak to this Gobbleguts.'

'Yes!' Inji felt a rush of excitement. These Scarlequins sounded dangerous, exotic, mysterious. Everything she had ever wanted to be. 'Please can we come too? I would love to see them. So would the boys, wouldn't you?'

Glyph nodded his head fiercely and Sil copied, although Inji wasn't sure he knew what he was agreeing to.

'Of course you can!' Pyewacket shouted, before Sheba could say anything. 'I'll drop you lot off at home, and then go and see if I can find out where the next show is. Our trusty Gutter Brigade will be on it like butter on a hot crumpet . . . I'll know by teatime.'

Sheba sighed. She still seemed troubled by the events in the pub, but mention of her old friends had brought the trace of a smile back. 'Very well,' she said. 'But we'll be going there to speak to Mr Gobbleguts, not gawp at the performances. And *definitely* not to think about joining them.' This last was said with a pointed glance at Inji.

Inji nodded, hard. She almost felt like laughing, but didn't in case Sheba took it the wrong way. Leave the home she had just found? For another sideshow circus? Inji didn't care if they were the most magical troupe in the world . . . there was no way she was going to put herself and Sil on show again. Not even if P. T. Barnum himself came calling.[viii] No, she was staying just where she was, and for as long as she possibly could.

*

Lunch was the most important thing on Sil's mind, and as soon as they got back, Sheba served them with loaves of bread, slabs of crumbly cheese and several slices of thick ham, juicy and pink.

The others hadn't seen the horrors within Skinker's chamber. They set to like starved animals, as if they hadn't just had a colossal breakfast a few hours earlier. Inji's appetite wasn't quite the same. She picked and nibbled, then pushed her plate aside.

Sheba had vanished somewhere. The house was silent. Sil had already made for the pile of blankets, clutching his stuffed belly. Glyph pulled out a deck of battered playing cards from one of his jacket's many pockets and began a game of patience. What was there for her to do except daydream of a life as an investigator for the Carnival? That, and to try to blank out the pictures of Skinker in his chair, the waxy look of horror on his frozen face. It was funny to think that, just a few days ago, she had spent several hours of every day wishing Skinker was dead. Now he was, and at the hands of the Hunters' Club, she didn't feel the slightest bit pleased. Instead, she was seething with hatred for those faceless enemies. They had tried to hurt her, and her brother. They had turned her life upside down, just to entertain their cruel desires. They hunted her kind like animals. What made people think they could behave so horribly?

And she still had no idea who they were, other than one of them had a red moustache. It was so frustrating. She could feel her anger swooshing around her body with nowhere to go. If she didn't let it out soon, she might burst . . .

'Here.' Sheba broke her daydreaming, bustling into the kitchen with an armful of clothes. 'These are some of mine and Pyewacket's old things. There should be plenty that will fit you all.' She paused behind Glyph and sniffed the air. 'And you all need a good bath. I'll fetch the tub.'

'Don't you have a maid?' Inji asked. Sheba had dumped the clothing on the kitchen floor. There were skirts and trousers, shirts, waistcoats, stockings and bloomers. All without a single patch or hole in them. 'I thought all posh people had maids.'

Sheba laughed. 'I wouldn't exactly call us posh. And we can manage fine by ourselves. Besides, I wouldn't want to ask someone to scrub Pyewacket's undergarments. There's probably a law against that kind of cruelty.'

Leaving them to sort through the pile, Sheba went to the scullery and dragged in a wide copper bathtub. Soon there were pots of water heating on the stove, and the three of them were busy measuring shirts and trousers up against themselves, as if they were gentlefolk in a tailor's shop.

There were several beautiful skirts and dresses that Inji politely turned down. Every colour of silk with matching petticoats and ribbons. But how would she climb and jump in one of those? In the end, she went for a pair of black tweed trousers, a grey collarless shirt and a waistcoat with lots of pockets. You could never have too many pockets.

Glyph refused to be parted from his velvet jacket, but picked out some short trousers and a clean shirt. As for Sil, there was nothing to fit his lumps and bumps. Once the bath was ready, Sheba began unpicking the seams of garments and sewing them together into something new and Sil-sized. Her long, thin fingers were quick and nimble. Inji could imagine them busy in her workshop, easily fitting cogs and gears into complex machines. It made her feel sorry for her own claw-tipped fingers. All they were good for was scratching and scraping. They caught on everything, even left snags on the china-doll dresses. *I'll never be an elegant lady like Sheba*, she thought, hiding her hands behind her back.

Soon enough, the water was hot, and the kitchen was filled with splashes, suds and scrubbing. By the time Pyewacket arrived back, there were three finely dressed children sitting in the parlour, their freshly combed hair leaving damp patches on their clean, pressed clothes.

'Blimey,' he said. 'What happened to those raggle-taggle tearaways what stumbled in off the streets? This lot looks like proper misses and masters. We shall have to hire a governess and a nanny to wipe their bottoms and blow their noses.'

'You could do with one to blow *your* nose,' said Inji.

'Blow it?' Pyewacket looked shocked. 'I never blow my nose. I might disrupt the workings of my amazing brain. I might spoil my next idea for a world-changing household product. I can feel the thoughts fermenting up there now: plates made of pastry to save on washing up. Self-cleaning underpants. Bits of paper with a sticky edge for writing notes on. Liquorice shoes in case you get hungry when you're walking . . .'

'Pyewacket!' Sheba snapped. 'Stop talking rubbish about your imaginary business. Did you find out about the Scarlequins?'

'Of course! What do you think I am – an amateur?' Pyewacket stuck his tongue out at Sheba before continuing. 'The Gutter Brigade have come up trumps again. Just so happens, the Scarlequins is putting on a show tonight! At a place called the Pigeon Court in St Giles. It's a bit hard to find, apparently, but Scribbles and Snatcher said they would meet us later and show us the way. What do you reckon, nippers? Fancy a trip to the circus?'

'Yes!' Inji shouted, while Glyph clapped his hands. Sil was tracing the patterns on a doily with his stubby fingers, but paused to pat his legs in glee.

'St Giles is a dangerous part of town,' said Sheba. 'If I'd known the venue was *there*, I would have suggested the two of us attending alone . . .'

Pyewacket laughed, clapping his hands like the others. 'Well, it's too late for that, isn't it? We already said they could go.'

'Yes.' The frown on Sheba's face was enough to make Inji stop celebrating for a moment. She was staring at them like a parent whose children have been invited to a tea party at a murderer's house. 'Yes, I'm afraid we did.'

*

Inji had heard of St Giles. Whispers on the streets, the mutterings of Skinker and his cronies. She knew it was a rookery: an area of old, tumbledown buildings, packed with half-starved families. A refuge for the most bloodthirsty gangs and criminals in the city. A place where no policeman would ever dare set foot, where a full purse could cost you your life, where the shirt on your back wasn't safe. A maze of secret alleys and crooked streets, the whole thing awash with rubbish heaps and foul air.

The worst part of it ran from below Great Russell Street along to the church of St Giles in the Fields. That fine building had begun its life as a colony of lepers, safely cut off from the rest of town by marshes and bogs. Now the churchyard was overflowing with dead bodies, the smart townhouses of a hundred years ago crumbling into rubble. Death and disease had come back to claim it, and the poor folk who lived there were too miserable to notice.

Even Skinker wouldn't set foot there, which was a very, very bad sign. And now they were all walking in, bold as brass. *Perhaps we should have listened to Sheba*, Inji thought. *Perhaps Pyewacket is a bit of a fool.* She'd realised that already, of course, but then her life hadn't been depending on one of his decisions.

It was early evening, the sun just setting and the gaslights being lit, making sputtering haloes of yellow light in the dirty fog. Not in St Giles, though. The narrow streets were already choked with shadow. The odd candle glimmered in a window, but otherwise gloom was everywhere. Entering that place was like stepping across a boundary into another world. One of darkness, foul smells and hidden blades. They stood on High Holborn, looking in.

'I was just wondering,' said Pyewacket, 'whether maybe, on second thoughts . . .'

'You promised them a circus,' said Sheba. 'So a circus they shall have.'

'Yes, but . . .'

Inji peered up at Pyewacket from beneath her shawl. Under the low brim of his bowler hat, he had gone quite pale. Sheba, on the other hand, looked fearless, determined. Like a battleship about to cruise into enemy waters.

'I'm sure we'll be fine,' she said. 'After all, I am armed to the teeth.'

Not that it showed. She wore a simple black dress with a matching woollen peacoat. A plain felt hat sat on her head, held in place with a few hairpins. Her jewellery and purse were gone; all she clutched was a small umbrella. *Every one of those things is probably a lethal weapon*, Inji thought, finding the idea very comforting. If only *she* had been allowed something. A pistol, or a poison-tipped knife, perhaps.

'Which way to the Pigeon Court?' Sheba asked.

'Let's ask our guides,' Pyewacket said. He pointed at two scruffy urchins, standing in the shadows of a doorway. Inji recognised them instantly. One was the boy with extraordinarily long fingers she had shouted to as she was being kidnapped. The other was one of the girls who had chased the cart. A thin tail hung down from beneath her skirt, curling around one ankle.

'Hello, Scribbles. Hello, Snatcher,' said Sheba. The children gave her a shy smile. 'Have you found out where this Pigeon Court is?'

'It's in the rookery,' said the girl. 'On one of the rooftops.'

'You can climb up from anywhere,' said the boy. 'But there's a ladder hidden in Bainbridge Street.'

The girl reached into her apron and pulled out a crumpled piece of paper. 'We drew you a map,' she said. 'On account of us not wanting to go in *there*.' She pointed deeper into the rookery, her eyes wide and frightened.

'That's very kind of you,' said Sheba, taking the map. 'Run off home, now. The others will be worried about you.'

'Yes, ma'am,' they both said together. They gave a muddle of bows and curtsies and then scurried off, running away from the rookery streets as fast as they could.

'I think it's best we avoid as much of St Giles as possible,' said Sheba. 'Can you all climb?'

'Sil and I can,' said Inji. 'Glyph might need a hand.'

With a nod, Sheba walked forward, looking for a suitable building to scale. The others hurried after, not wanting to be left even a footstep behind.

People, Inji thought. *So many people.* They thronged the pavements and clogged the road. Men and women, all stooped and haggard, hidden under layers of filthy clothing. They lounged in doorways, hung out of windows and milled in loose crowds all over the place. They moaned and muttered to each other. Some were playing dice or cards, some arm-wrestling or trying to peddle stolen pieces of silk and silver. Most had a clay bottle or tin cup in their hands, and Inji could smell the sharp, sour stink of gin, even over the stench of the filthy streets.

Gangs of children swarmed everywhere, dashing in between legs, clambering over mounds of rotting rubbish. They threw jagged shards of pot and old bricks at each other, screaming with laughter, especially when someone got hit.

Three tatty, soot-smeared creatures were chasing a cat, pelting it with bits of rotten wood. The poor animal streaked past Inji, hissing. She could see the ragged thing's ribs, and gouges in its patchy fur where it had already been hit. The sight made her hackles rise. There was no way she could let this pass.

You keep on running, sister, she thought. *I've got this one.*

She stepped in front of the cat's pursuers, tripping one over with her foot. The other two rounded on her, fierce eyes staring out from matted clumps of filthy hair. Inji couldn't tell if they were boys or girls. They looked more like wild animals, shrieking at her in their odd street language, raising their clods of wood to target her instead. She pulled back her shawl and *hissed*, showing them her needle teeth and slitted eyes. Knowing danger when they saw it, they scampered off, looking for a smaller victim to torture.

'Don't get involved,' Sheba whispered to her. 'Not even for a cat.'

Eyes were on them now. Bloodshot stares from whiskered faces beneath battered top hats. One or two figures shifted from their huddled groups, hands moving into coat pockets where knives and cudgels were hidden.

'Down this alley,' Sheba whispered. 'Quick as you can.'

They ducked between two collapsing houses, propped up against each other by a lattice of rotting timbers.

'Pyewacket, take Glyph.' Sheba lifted the boy up on to her friend's back and he was away in a blink, leaping from strut to strut with an effortless ease. *Almost graceful*, Inji had to admit.

'Will Sil be able to climb?' Sheba asked. She was bending down to twist the heels of her knee-length leather boots. Inji saw the glint of steel spikes clicking out from the soles.

'Of course,' she said. Then, to her brother, 'Sil, we're going up. Up to the chimneys.'

'Chimneys,' said Sil, and grabbed the nearest timber. He swung himself on to the wall, then began punching his own handholds.

Crump, crump, crump. Up he went, almost as fast as Pyewacket, and just in time: the silhouettes of five figures had appeared at the alley entrance, sauntering towards them. Like a sheep being approached by a pack of wolves, Inji was filled with the sudden urge to flee.

'Are you coming?' she said to Sheba, not wanting to leave her.

Sheba grinned, her canine teeth sparkling. She held up her hands to show clawed fingernails. 'Race you,' she said.

Grinning back, Inji leapt on to the wall. The brick was soft, crumbly with age. Her claws sank into it easily as she pushed off with her powerful legs, leaping upwards in a series of stretching bounds. Three, four, five leaps and she had reached the rooftop, perching on the edge like a true cat and staring down into the dark alley below.

Sheba was about halfway up; moving fast, but not a patch on Inji's speed, the catgirl was pleased to note. Sheba's spiked boots dug into the bricks and woodwork, her clawed hands searched for cracks and ledges to hold. The thugs in the alleyway were pointing up and shouting insults, but were too far away to do any harm. The others were on the roof behind Inji, Glyph still clinging to Pyewacket's back.

Inji took a moment to look around at the sea of chimney pots and rooftops, stretching off into the distance. She could see the spire of St Giles's church, and the orange glow of the sunset in between the threads of smoke from a thousand, thousand chimneys. From up here, even a rookery didn't look too bad.

'Well done, Inji.' Sheba was finally at the top, clambering over the roof edge. The spikes of her shoes bit into the slate, allowing her to stand up without sliding. She took a moment to catch her breath. 'I suppose cats make better climbers than wolves. I'll give you that.'

'Pigeons,' said Sil. He pointed to a spot a few rooftops away, where a cloud of birds was spiralling. They could see the silhouettes of people there, dancing in and out of the chimney stacks, while the sound of music drifted over to them, through the smoke. The scene looked like a gathering of forest fairies, completely out of place on the London rooftops, yet perfectly suited at the same time.

'The Pigeon Court,' said Inji. 'Well spotted, Sil.' Her excitement at seeing the Scarlequins bubbled up, even after all the horror of the rookery.

'Here we are then,' said Pyewacket, his cheery grin returning. 'Just as I promised. It's circus time, boys and girls. Let's not be late!'

Chapter Eight

In which the Carnival meet a survivor of the Hunters' Club.

'Roll up! Roll up! Take your seats, ladles and jellyspoons!'

Skipping and slithering over the rooftops, the Carnival made their way to the Pigeon Court just as the last call was being made.

Inji noticed one or two others picking their way between the chimneys to where a crowd of fifty or so already sat, perched on old crates and upturned rusty buckets that had been laid out in a rough circle on the flat-topped roof of what was once a proud Georgian townhouse.

Strings of paper lanterns and bunting had been

looped around chimney stacks and tied to rickety poles. As Inji got closer, she could see everything was made from bits of rubbish: scraps of hessian sacking and old newspapers, stubs of candles and cracked jam jars. But instead of looking tatty, the whole scene had a strange kind of fairy-tale beauty.

The rest of the audience were folk very similar to those they had just seen in the rookery below. They all wore clothing held together with patches and pins. The men wore top hats that were battered and squashed. The women had layers of filthy shawls and torn felt bonnets. There were children too, half-starved wildlings with wide eyes and hollow cheeks. They reminded Inji of how she and Sil had looked, when they had lived on the streets.

They followed Sheba as she hopped up to the Court rooftop and took a seat on a long wooden crate. There was a wide chimney stack behind them, buried in thick layers of pigeon poo. There must have been a century's worth, all piled in crumbly cakes. Weeds and wildflowers with pretty pink petals had started to sprout from it. Sil pressed his hands against the cracked brickwork and stared up at the wisps of smoke curling into the sky.

Inji sat down too, her eyes scanning the scene for Gobbleguts or Sheba's old friends. She noticed a tent set up in a corner of the rooftop. A torn and battered thing with its guy ropes held down by lumps of old brick. She guessed the acts were waiting inside.

'Dig deep, my friends! Reach into those pockets! Time to pay the piper!'

The same voice that had been calling to the crowd sounded again, and Inji spotted its owner: a tall lady, as thin as a willow, with long silver hair loose down her back. She wore a frock coat that reached to her knees, with frills of silk cuffs spilling out of the sleeves. It was made of an unusual patchwork: diamond lozenges of faded material that looked like pieces of old skirts and curtains. Rather than a dress, she wore trousers and knee-high leather boots painted with gold squiggles and spirals.

As she got closer, Inji could see a narrow, delicate face; snow-pale skin and sharp eyes that seemed to sparkle with stolen secrets. They were the same colour as her hair – a light grey flecked with glints of silver.

And then Inji saw her neck – it was marked on the left side, from ear to shoulder, with a pattern of criss-cross scars. Deliberate slices that had healed into raised lines of scar tissue, in shapes just like the diamonds that decorated her coat.

'Welcome to the Pigeon Court,' she was saying to the people sitting in front. 'Your payment, please.'

'That's the Marquess,' Sheba whispered in Inji's ear. 'She runs the Scarlequins. Watch everything you say to her.'

'Is she the one who ran away and formed the troupe?' Inji asked.

'Don't be daft,' said Pyewacket, who had unfortunately chosen to sit next to her. 'That was a hundred years ago!'

'Even so,' said Sheba. 'It wouldn't surprise me.'

Inji stared as the Marquess took payment from her patrons. There were coins, scraps of silk, ornaments of copper and china. Some gave her tiny parcels wrapped in brown paper, some tattered envelopes, others chipped and cracked objects still coated in the river mud they had been scooped from.

One or two leaned over to whisper in her ear.

Everything she was given disappeared into the deep pockets of her coat with a flick of her long, nimble fingers. The secret words whispered to her were accepted with a smile and a nod.

And then she was standing in front of them, her eyes twinkling. 'Ah,' she said. 'The Carnival of the Lost. We are honoured, indeed.'

'Marquess,' said Sheba, her voice a touch cold. She held out a handful of coins, which the Marquess quickly pocketed.

'Most generous,' she said. 'Come to see your friends? Or bringing me some new recruits?' Her silver gaze fell on Inji, who was trying hard not to stare at her scarred neck.

'These are *not* for you,' Sheba said, her eyes flashing.

'We shall see,' the Marquess laughed, glints of candlelight sparking silver in her hair as she shook her head. 'We shall see.'

And then she was gone into the crowd, collecting more gifts.

'I forgot how creepy she was,' Pyewacket said.

Sheba nodded. Inji had felt it too. If she'd ever had any thoughts about running away and joining the circus, they were gone for good now. Seeing those scars on the Marquess had sent a deep chill through her bones.

'And I didn't ask her about Gobbleguts,' said

Sheba. 'We shall have to wait until after the show.'

Inji was about to point out the tent and suggest they could try and sneak their way in, when she was interrupted by a high-pitched squeaking from somewhere under her feet. She bent over, peering at the bottom of the packing crate they sat on, where a large hole had been gnawed through the planks.

Something rustled and chittered inside the box. She caught a glimpse of oily fur, the flick of a scaly tail. 'Rat!' On instinct, in a flash, she pulled her feet up and moved into a crouch. Her claws dug into the crate and bristly hair stood on end all over her body.

She felt a hand on her back. It was Sheba, and she was smiling. 'Relax, Inji. I think you'll find it's a friendly one.'

'A friendly rat?' Inji found it difficult to speak in human tones. The cat inside her head was going crazy. It wanted to smash the crate to splinters and get to the juicy rat inside, as if it was a Christmas present in wooden wrapping.

'Hello?' Sheba called, bending down to the hole. 'Who's there?'

There was another squeak, and a furry head appeared. Patchy grey fur, with milky eyes. Its whiskers quivered and shook as it stuck its nose from the crate to sniff the air. It was the oldest rat Inji had ever seen.

'It's Paul!' Sheba said, nudging Pyewacket. He looked about as pleased to see the thing as Inji did.

'Hello, Paul,' he said, and then muttered under his breath. Inji caught the words 'diseased' and 'vermin'.

Squeak, squeak, went Paul. If it was possible, the rat sounded annoyed.

'Ignore him,' said Sheba, apparently to the rat. 'You remember what he's like. Does Mama Rat know we're here?'

The rat nodded. It poked two shaky paws from the hole and waved them in the air.

'She'll see us after the show?' Sheba translated. The rat nodded again. It raised its nose to Inji and did something with its eye that might have been a wink, and then it disappeared.

'Did . . . did that rat just talk to you?' Inji was still crouched on the crate, ready to pounce.

'Oh yes,' said Sheba. 'That was one of Mama Rat's furry friends. I've known him since he was a baby.

He's ten years old now, would you believe it?'

'No. No, I wouldn't.' Inji's cat mind was full of the urge to chase after the thing. Follow it back to its nest and rip everything to pieces. *Stop it*, she told herself. *Be still now. The rat's . . . a friend. I think.*

With an effort, she managed to slow her breathing and sit back down. Pyewacket was chuckling away next to her.

'Should have let catgirl eat the disgusting thing,' he said. 'Mind you, might be a bit stringy.'

'Hush, Pyewacket,' said Sheba. 'The show is starting.'

Inji looked up to see the last rays of sunlight disappear behind the spires and chimneys to the west. She just had time to pull Sil over to his seat before a circle of bullseye lanterns (that looked suspiciously like they had been 'borrowed' from several policemen) were lit, flooding the centre of the rooftop with their yellow beams.

'Look, Sil,' she whispered. 'The circus has come to town.'

*

Inji had been a part of many shows, of course, but they had been in front of little more than a crowd of drunken idiots screaming at a stage. *This* was a proper performance. *This* was a spectacle. It was like theatre, ballet and storybook all mixed together into a magic spell.

The Marquess was on first. She had changed out of her coat and trousers and into a one-piece outfit, covered in that criss-cross diamond pattern. A mask hid her nose and eyes, and her mane of hair was brushed until it stood up like a lion's, silver strands glinting in the spotlights.

She raised her arms to the crowd, and then bowed low before launching into a routine of flips, spins and cartwheels, each movement performed with perfect balletic grace. Somewhere in the shadows behind her, a fiddle played a sad song, matching her steps exactly. Inji held her breath as she watched, feeling as though she was being told a fairy tale in sound and dance. A sad one, full of loneliness and longing. The story of every sideshow player, made to perform for a jeering mob each night, yet never fit to walk among them or even speak to them. Always apart, always alone . . .

When the Marquess took her bow at the end, tears

were spilling down Inji's cheeks. She stole a glance at Sheba and saw her dabbing her eyes with a kerchief.

After that came the other acts. There was a fire eater who blew clouds of flame into the air, sending flocks of pigeons flapping for safety. A sword swallower who walked on his hands with three sabres jutting from his mouth. An old man of sixty or seventy who was the size of a toddler, and who played a miniature set of bagpipes so fast, his tiny fingers were a blur.

Some of the performers were very skilled human beings. Others were … *different* … like Inji and her friends. But none of the crowd ever jeered or laughed, let alone threw bottles. There was an understanding here. There was respect. *This is how it should be*, Inji thought. *Everybody being accepted just the way they are.*

When the tent opened and a colossal, muscled man stepped out, the crowd cheered and whooped.

'Gigantus!' Pyewacket shouted. 'He's not as tough as he looks, everybody! He writes books about petticoats and blouses!'

Gigantus was the tallest, widest person Inji had ever seen. His shirt and waistcoat strained to hold in the slabs of muscle that were stacked from his neck to his toes. His shaved head was covered with the lines of old scars, but under his heavy brow, his eyes were gentle. As he began to lift members of the audience above his head one-handed, Inji noticed there were fresh wounds on the back of his neck. A pattern of crossed lines that made diamonds, the same as the cuts on the Marquess. *Does everyone who joins the Scarlequins have to be marked?* she wondered. She was glad the Carnival didn't have any such strange and painful traditions.

After Gigantus took his final bow, a familiar face stepped into the circle of light. Inji instantly recognised the stooped, scrawny figure of Gobbleguts. He had waxy, pale skin, a spattering of thin hair and an enormously wide mouth that took up most of his face. Even though he ate enough food in one meal to feed six families, he was always gaunt and doubled over, as if his belly hurt him. Which, considering the things he put into it, it probably did.

Tonight, he had a whole dead pig laid out before him. As the crowd stared in stunned silence, he began to rip the flesh from the animal and gulp it down, raw. It was like watching some kind of wild beast devour its prey. Within a few minutes, the skin and muscle were gone, and Gobbleguts had started on the bones. Most of them he swallowed whole, but the big ones were cracked in his powerful jaws before being scoffed. He sucked out the eyeballs and smashed the skull to bits on the rooftop before shovelling the pieces into his gullet. In less than ten minutes, the whole pig was gone.

The crowd was too stunned to give more than a quiet ripple of applause before he waddled off, clutching his belly, which was now round, fat and full of dead pig. Inji's sharp eyes spotted the edge of a fresh bandage on his left arm, just peeking out from his sleeve. She wondered if it was covering a set of diamond scratches – the marks that showed Gobbleguts was now a Scarlequin.

The last act was a woman who could only be Mama Rat. She was a middle-aged lady with long chestnut hair that hung in ringlets, streaked with strands of grey. A broad-brimmed hat hid her eyes in shadow, but she had a delicate nose and wide, full lips. In another setting, in another life, she might have been one of those people who drew every gaze in the ballroom. Now, however, her six black-furred rats were the stars.

She had a tiny circus ring set up for them, with tightropes, trapezes and a trampoline. They performed amazing feats of acrobatics on a miniature scale, flipping and zipping all over the place. Throughout it all, Paul – the ancient rat that had 'spoken' to them earlier – stood watch, clapping his knobbled paws. He was dressed in a ringmaster's uniform, complete with scarlet coat and top hat. Where it might have been cute on any other creature, on Paul the effect was quite unsettling. Besides which, Inji couldn't really enjoy the show when every instinct she had was telling her to rip the stars into bleeding pieces.

They finished up by making a teetering ratty pyramid, to much applause from the audience. The Marquess appeared from the shadows, bowing and waving, and then the circus was over.

'That,' said Inji, 'was *amazing*.'

Sil and Glyph were still clapping their hands long after the rest of the crowd had begun to drift away. Soon it was just the Carnival left, sitting on their crate as the acts emerged from the tent to start packing everything up.

Two figures moved away from the rest, stepping over the boxes and buckets, making straight for Sheba and the others. It was Gigantus and Mama Rat, both with wide smiles of welcome on their faces.

'Sheba! Pyewacket! Paul told me you were here,' said Mama Rat. 'It's so good to see you, my dearies.'

She held out her arms and wrapped them both in a tight hug. Gigantus did the same, almost crushing the life out of Pyewacket.

'Take it easy, you big ape,' said Pyewacket, gasping for breath. 'If you squeeze me too hard, you never know what'll come out!'

'As disgusting as ever, I see,' said Gigantus. His voice was like a grizzly bear's growl, echoing through its underground cave. He gave Pyewacket a slap on the back that sent him flying over the packing crate to smack into the chimney stack and then crumple to a heap on the floor. Glyph and Sil fell about laughing.

'And who are these three sweet dears?' Mama Rat asked. She held out her hand for Inji and Glyph to shake. Sil shied away, but Mama Rat smiled at him all the same.

'They are . . . helping us with our enquiries,' said Sheba. 'Have you heard of the Hunters' Club murders?'

'Sideshow acts being kidnapped and killed?' Mama Rat's smile disappeared. 'How could we not have heard? It's simply awful. Everyone here is terrified. In fact, there's talk about leaving the city. At least until it blows over.'

'Are you going after them?' Gigantus asked. He balled one giant hand into a clublike fist and cradled it with the other. 'I'm tempted to join you. I would love to have a crack at whoever's doing it.'

'Why don't you join us, then?' Pyewacket asked, picking himself up from the floor and brushing clods of pigeon poo from his clothes. 'We could use some muscle. And … er … some rodents.'

'I wish we could,' said Mama Rat. 'But I'm not sure the Marquess would approve. And the secret life of the Scarlequins suits us better. We're getting too old to go running around town, capturing villains.'

'I suppose Marie is right,' said Gigantus. 'Besides, the Scarlequins need our protection. If those hunters want people like us as their victims … well, they'll have hit the jackpot if they discover our troupe. We nearly didn't perform tonight because of them. The sooner we move on, the better.'

'Sorry, Sheba,' said Mama Rat. 'Besides, I don't think you really need any more bodies. Not with all your skills and gadgets. *And* these new recruits of yours. I'm sure those horrible hunters don't stand a chance.'

'Actually,' said Sheba. 'They are the reason we came here tonight. We need to speak to Gobbleguts, you see. He escaped the hunters, and we think he might be able to identify them for us.'

'He did, did he?' Mama Rat looked over at the tent where the other acts were gathered. 'He kept that quiet. But I did sense he came here to get away from some kind of trouble. Wait right there . . . I'll go and fetch him for you.'

Mama Rat turned to where the other acts were gathered and gave a shrill whistle. A few seconds later, the stooped form of Gobbleguts came shuffling over. He was being herded towards them by six fat, greasy black rats scampering and nipping at his feet. Inji bit back a yowl and dug her claws into her palms, forcing herself to stand still. *Steady, girl . . . steady . . .*

'Ouch!' Gobbleguts hopped to and fro. 'What's all this about? I'm trying to digest, you know. If you wanted to speak to me, you only had to ask! Call them off! Call them off!'

'Thank you, my dearies,' said Mama Rat. Her pets squeaked back at her and then scuttered off to the other side of the rooftop. Inji let out the breath she had been holding.

'Inji? Sil? Is that you? I haven't seen you since that half-faced cove bought you from Pasternak! What are you doing here?' Gobbleguts didn't exactly look pleased to see them. More confused, and a bit frightened. He was much pastier than Inji remembered. There were dark shadows under his eyes, and he kept casting quick glances over his shoulder, as if there might be someone creeping up behind him.

He still had that horrible stink about him, though. Like the drains behind a butcher's shop that specialised in rotten elephant meat. And he was drenched in greasy sweat like he always was after one of his 'meals'. It looked like boiled fat was leaking out of his pores.

'We were sold on by Skinker,' Inji said. 'To some rotter with a fox mask who shoved us in a crate. I think you know who I'm talking about.'

Inji's words made the blood drain from Gobbleguts's face. His eyes boggled in terror. 'No, not them! Why have you come here? What if they followed you? What if they're here now?'

'Relax, Mr Gobbleguts,' said Sheba. 'We're trying

to find out who did this. We want to stop them, bring them to justice. But we need all the information we can get. We were hoping you would answer a few questions for us.'

'Questions? No! I have to go! I have to go now!'

He turned to run, but suddenly the slender form of the Marquess was there, blocking his path. She had changed back into her frock coat and trousers and was staring at them all with those eerie silver eyes.

'Stay where you are, Gobbleguts,' she said. 'Nobody'd dare hurt you while I'm around. Now. Is what I just heard true? You lot are going after the Hunters' Club?'

Sheba nodded. 'We're trying to. Gobbleguts is the only person who has survived capture by them. We need to find out what he knows.'

The Marquess laid a hand on Gobbleguts's shoulder, calming him down but also stopping him from leaving. 'Tell them what you know,' she said to him. 'Every last detail. If anyone can catch these monsters, it's Sheba and her friends.'

Gobbleguts swallowed and clutched his bulging, gurgling belly as if to comfort himself. 'Very well. I'll tell. If you think it'll help.'

'It will,' said Inji. 'You can trust us.'

Gobbleguts nodded. He closed his eyes and began his tale.

'It was Pasternak that sold us. Me and Benjamin. To a posh gent with proper smart clothes. He had ginger hair and big mutton-chop whiskers that joined up under his hooter.

'At first we were excited. He gave us a ride in his carriage, even fed us grapes and chocolate. We thought we were going off to some upmarket show. A proper exhibition or a museum. Maybe even to live in a hospital and get studied. The good life. Except we soon realised something was wrong. We pulled up at an old warehouse, and he made us get out of the carriage. We went inside, into an empty room with just this big crate in, and then … that was it. Somebody grabbed me from behind and pressed a cloth to my mouth. It stank of a horrible chemical. My head went all woozy and I blacked out.'

'Chloroform,'[ix] said Sheba. 'They didn't want you to know where you were going.'

'Well, we had no idea about that, or anything else,' said Gobbleguts. 'We were snuffed out like ha'penny candles.' His whole body was beginning to shake as he got to the most terrifying part of his story. 'When I woke up, I was in a cage in some sort of cellar. It was damp and gloomy, and there were no windows to peep out of.

'Bendylegs was there as well. Frightened out of our wits we were, the pair of us. And then it got worse. These men came in: five of them, I think. All wearing leather coats and with these masks made of animal heads. Foxes and wolves . . . one looked like a tiger or leopard. Their eyes were hidden behind dark goggles. You couldn't see any part of their face at all.

'That was when we both started screaming, but these hunters . . . they just laughed. They dragged us out of the cage and tied blindfolds over our eyes. We were hauled out of the cellar. I remember feeling steps going up, then floorboards. We went through one or two doorways, and then we were outside. I felt gravel under my feet, then grass, then roots and dead leaves.

'Finally, they stopped us and pulled the blindfolds off. We were in a wood, and it was night-time. I remember the moon being full, and really bright. You could see it shining through the branches above.

'The hunters were all there, and they had weapons. Crossbows, I think you call them. One of them had a spear. "Welcome to the hunt," says the one with fox ears. "We hope you have as much fun as we do." Then they all laughed again. Then another one says, "Gwydion, when will your new bows be ready? These old things weigh a ton." It was like they were about to have a tea party. Not planning to kill two poor, harmless souls.

'Benjamin and me, we were pleading and begging by now, but they just laughed some more. Then the wolf-eared one shoves us off the path. "You have a ten-minute start," he says. "Don't waste it."

'I don't know what happened to Benjamin, but I ran like the hounds of hell were after me. My feet have never moved so fast in my life. I crashed through trees and bushes until I came to a lake . . . fell into it, actually.

'I knew I couldn't swim fast enough to get away. They'd have seen me splashing around and shot me. So I headed to a bank where there were lots of reeds and rushes. I opened my mouth wide and swallowed as much water as I could (which is a lot). Enough to make me sink right down. I kept my mouth just below the surface, so I could snatch a breath every now and then, and I stayed there. I didn't move until the sun was in the sky, because I figured those hunters wouldn't want to walk around in broad daylight, dressed up like that.

'I poked my head out and couldn't see them, so I followed the bank of the lake until I came to a stream. I waded up that for a bit, then walked through some fields. I could see London, off to the south, so that's where I headed, catching a ride on a hop cart most of the way. When I got into town, I went straight to Pasternak, thinking she would want to know there had been a mistake. But she was just as afraid as me. Told me to clear off. She must have known what that evil toff was up to all along.'

'And then he found us, and we took him in,' finished the Marquess. 'Well done, Gobbleguts. That must have been hard for you.'

'This place they took you,' said Sheba. 'Would you be able to locate it for us?'

Gobbleguts shook his head. 'I only know it was somewhere north. A big house, I guess, from what I could make out. A manor or a castle.'

'What about the man who bought you?' Inji said. 'Would you be able to spot him again?'

'Spot him?' Gobbleguts began to shake violently,

moving as close to the Marquess as he could. 'I never want to see him again! We're leaving this place as soon as we can, aren't we? Aren't we?'

'Shh,' said the Marquess. 'Yes, we're leaving.' She held up one of her long-fingered hands to Sheba and Inji. 'I think that's enough questions,' she said. 'This poor man has been through a terrible ordeal . . .'

'Yes, but he's the only one who can finger this bloke with the red tash,' said Pyewacket. 'We can use Gobbleguts to prove he's part of the Hunters' Club!'

'You won't be using him for anything,' said the Marquess. 'As of tonight, we are leaving for Edinburgh. It just isn't safe for our kind in this city any more. We wish you luck in finding these villains. Perhaps if you do, it will be safe for us to come back.'

'But . . .' Inji began. The Marquess simply shook her head and sketched out an elaborate bow. Then she led Gobbleguts away, to where her other acts had almost finished packing up the circus.

'I'm sorry about that,' said Mama Rat. 'I hope it was of some use to you.'

'It was no use!' Sheba cried. 'He hasn't told us

anything we didn't know already! Our only hope was that he'd help us identify Red Moustache Man, and he can't do that if he's at the other end of the country!'

'You know their hunting ground is a manor house north of London,' said Gigantus.

'And there was that name he heard,' said Inji. 'Gwydion, or some such . . .'

'That's not enough,' said Sheba. She wrung her hands together and stared after Gobbleguts. 'I was hoping for a better lead. A solid clue . . .'

'That's all we've got, Sheebs,' said Pyewacket. 'It's better than nothing. You'll find a way to use it, you always do.'

Sheba gave a deep sigh. 'I suppose,' she said.

'Come on,' said Gigantus. 'I'll walk you out of the rookery.'

The big man led them to a stairwell and back down into the streets of St Giles. The crowds of lolling people were still there, slightly more drunk than before, but just as hostile. However, when they saw Gigantus, they parted like ice before a steamship. None of them dared even raise their eyes from the pavement.

'It was nice seeing you again,' Gigantus said, as

he left them safely on High Holborn. 'We'll keep in touch. And once this all blows over, hopefully we'll come back to town.'

'I hope so,' said Sheba. 'We don't see enough of you.'

Gigantus gave both Pyewacket and Sheba another bone-crushing hug, then bent down to shake Inji and Glyph's hands. Inji's whole arm was almost swallowed up by his enormous fist.

'Take care of these ones,' he said. 'They remind me of you two, when you were both little.' And then he turned and disappeared into the dark streets of the rookery.

'What now?' Inji asked Sheba. 'Is it all over? Have we given up?'

Sheba forced her mouth into a grim smile. 'We never give up. We just have to come up with a new plan.'

'We can do that tomorrow though, eh?' said Pyewacket. He pointed at Glyph, who was yawning so much, he looked like a miniature version of Gobbleguts.

'Yes,' said Sheba. 'Let's go home and to bed. We'll see what tomorrow brings.'

'It'll bring something useful,' Inji whispered, 'if

it knows what's good for it.' With a warning glance at the sky, where perhaps tomorrow was hiding, she pulled her shawl up over her head and followed the others home.

Chapter Nine

In which Sheba's gentleman friend comes calling.

'It *must* be one of these,' said Sheba. 'But which?'

They were in the workshop, where the far wall had been turned into a giant incident board. A huge map of London and the surrounding countryside had been pinned to the wall, and all the stately homes and manor houses north of the city marked with red pins. Most had pieces of twine tied around them, leading off to etchings of grand buildings – all pillars, crenellations and bay windows – set in rolling grounds with lashings of topiary, follies and ornamental ponds. They looked unreal to Inji. Like pictures from a fairy tale.

Sheba walked over to a stack of newspapers and pamphlets on her desk. She began tearing out pages, then going back to the wall and pasting them next to the house pictures with a splodge of thick yellow glue from a dripping brush.

When she was done, she stood back, chewing at her nails and frowning. She had been doing a lot of chewing and frowning, the past couple of days.

'What are you putting on there now?' Inji asked. From where she was standing it looked like more etchings, this time of people.

'These are portraits of the owners,' said Sheba. Without taking her eyes from the wall, she reached behind her and waved a magazine at Inji. 'All the ones I can find pictures of.'

Inji took the magazine from her and began flipping through. It was full of articles about high society balls and parties. Lists of who was there, what they had been wearing, who performed . . . even what kind of hors d'oeuvres had been served. Each article had a sketch alongside, showing gentlemen in long-tailed jackets and ladies wearing enough lace to supply a small country with tablecloths.

'Do you think Redtash might have been at one of these lah-di-dah shindigs?' Inji asked. She was torn between laughing at some of the ridiculous outfits and wishing she could go to one herself. To swirl around a polished floor in time to the music . . . To wear clothes that were clean and delicate and pretty, which didn't get ripped to shreds by her claws . . .

'Perhaps,' said Sheba, still chewing a finger. 'And if we can match him to one of these houses . . .'

'Then we might know where the Hunters' Club is based!' Inji finished. She moved nearer the wall, peering closely at each face Sheba had pasted. Most of the men did indeed have beards or whiskers or sideburns, but they were all drawn in black ink. There was no way of knowing whether any were red-haired or not.

'I've been to one or two of those balls,' Sheba muttered. 'But I can't remember anyone with red hair. I mean, some people must have had it, but I didn't notice . . .'

'How were you to know one might have been a murderous criminal?' Inji said, going back to the magazine. Now she wanted to find a picture of Sheba, all dressed up.

'It's the aristocracy, Inji. They're *all* murderous criminals.'

That made Inji chuckle. 'Who's to say Redtash is even a lord or baron? He might just be one of their butlers or servants. Someone to do their dirty work.'

'I've thought of that,' said Sheba. 'But a butler would not have that particular accent. Not unless he was pretending. We have to eliminate the possibility he could be an aristocrat first.'

Inji gave a frustrated sigh. Then she stopped flicking and peered at an etching of a group of finely dressed partygoers, frozen in mid-dance. 'Is this you?'

Sheba glanced at the picture and nodded, before quickly returning her attention to the board. Inji stared at the drawing of the elegant woman in the magazine. The artist had captured Sheba's dark curls perfectly; the shape of her neck, her dainty nose and those full lips. She had her eyes closed in the picture, as if lost in the pleasure of the dance. A tall young man with collar-length hair and cheekbones like razor blades was whisking her across the dance floor.

'Who's that?' Inji asked. 'The handsome fellow who's dancing with you?'

'That?' Sheba tried to hide the blush that was

creeping across her cheeks. 'Oh, that's just Lucas. I mean, Mr Garrow. He's the one who invited me there.'

'Oh,' said Inji. 'The posh relation who saved you from the sideshow.'

'Yes, that's him. When my father died and my mother disappeared on her voyage back from India, Lucas's family inherited our estate. But Lord Garrow was so rich, he mostly forgot about it. It was only when he decided to sell off this house that he sent Lucas to inspect it. And that's when he discovered me.'

'An estate? You have an estate?'

Sheba blushed again. 'Just this house, really. And a small manor on the Isle of Wight. Wolverton, it's called. Although it's nothing like the ones on the wall there. I hear the house has crumbled to the ground now, and the land is covered by reeds and marshes.'

'Still,' said Inji. 'An *estate.*' She gave a low whistle to show how impressive it sounded. Sheba gave her a gentle shove. 'And yet the lord still thinks you're not good enough for his son.'

'Hush about that!' Sheba frowned. 'I'm trying to think.'

Inji went back to staring at the image of Sheba, waltzing. She held her tongue for all of ten seconds.

'What's it like?' she asked. 'Being at a ball . . . dressed up . . . dancing . . .'

Sheba huffed and was about to say something scathing, then seemed to catch the look on Inji's face. That painful yearning for dreams that would never come true. Had she felt the same when she was a young, hair-covered girl, trapped in a cruel sideshow?

'It's not as incredible as you might think, Inji,' she said, her voice soft. 'In fact, it's not all that different from being in a penny sideshow. You're still paraded in front of people to be gawped at, except these ones don't openly shout insults and laugh at you. No, they're nice as pie to your face, and then they go off in their huddles and talk about you behind your back. They say worse things than a bunch of drunken dockmen. I heard them all, you know, with my wolf's ears.'

Inji looked at her feet, unable to meet Sheba's eyes. 'I didn't really want . . . I didn't think . . .'

Sheba smiled. 'I know. I know.' When Inji caught her eye again, she said, 'I used to have dreams of being normal too, you see. Of dancing in ball gowns and princes' castles. But once you take off this mask . . .' she ran a finger down Inji's furred cheek, 'you have to put on another. One that everybody in "pleasant" society seems to wear. And underneath it they are far, far uglier than we sideshow folk. At least we are honest with each other. And ourselves.'

Inji nodded. Yet the thought of being normal, even for an evening . . . Wanting to change the subject, she looked back at the wall, her eye catching on the name Gobbleguts had overheard: 'GWYDION'. Sheba had written it in capital letters on a piece of thick paper and pinned it to the centre of the map.

'What about that name?' Inji asked. 'Are there any toffs called that? If you can find out who *he* is and where he lives . . .'

'That was the first thing I tried,' said Sheba. 'And with no luck. No aristocrats with that as a first *or* last name.' She went over to a large, leather-bound book that lay open on her workbench.

'From what I can gather, Gwydion is a mythical character. He comes from the legend of the Wild Hunt.'

'The what?'

'The Wild Hunt.' Sheba lifted the book to show Inji a drawing of a horde of mounted riders, charging down from the sky, blowing horns and waving spears. 'It's a legend from old cultures all over

Europe. Some say they are devils, some say elves or fairies. They are supposed to come from another world, riding into this one to chase down their victims on dark, stormy nights. All very dramatic and terrifying.'

Inji scratched her chin. 'So you think these Hunters' Club coves are using names from old legends? Why would they do that?'

'It's what these rich men in their clubs do,' said Sheba, shaking her head. 'London is full of them: drinking clubs, eating clubs, gambling, fighting and racing clubs. All grown men, acting like spoilt, silly boys, with too much time on their hands. They form these groups, ban all women, then give themselves stupid names, rules and rituals to make themselves seem important. Honestly, it's like they're still in the playground at Eton.'

'And also, to keep their identities a secret,' said Inji. 'Because if Gobbleguts had heard their real names, we could be round there with the police right now.'

'Yes,' said Sheba. 'I suppose.'

She was about to go back to her wall when a bell began to ring somewhere in the house above.

'I'll get it!' Pyewacket shouted. Then, a moment

later, 'Sheba! Come up here! It's your special friend come to visit!'

'Mr Garrow?' Sheba instantly became flustered, patting at her hair and skirts. 'Why is he here? I wasn't expecting him!'

'You look fine,' said Inji. 'You look beautiful.'

'But this old dress ...' Sheba pulled off the apron she was wearing and threw it on to the bench, the tools in its pockets clattering and clanking.

'Shall I get Glyph and Sil and bring them down here?' Inji asked.

'What?' Sheba stopped her fussing and stared at Inji in surprise.

'Out of the way,' Inji explained. 'Skinker never liked us being about when he had visitors. In case we scared them off.'

'What nonsense!' Sheba grabbed her arm and started leading her up the stairs. 'I shall be proud to introduce you to Lucas. And as for me, he shall have to take me as I am. It will serve him right for not arranging a visit properly.'

*

By the time Inji and Sheba had dashed up the stairs, Pyewacket had shown Mr Garrow into the parlour. Voices could be heard within.

'Heavens above,' Sheba whispered. 'Hurry up, before that imp does something dreadful!'

They burst into the room, just as Pyewacket was in mid-speech. '. . . and I've spoken to several shopkeepers who I'm sure will be interested in selling my Poo Projectiles. I just need to perfect the recipe. I've been using a mixture of dog mess and horse dung, but I think – if I could get hold of some really stinky fox droppings – I could . . .'

'Pyewacket! That's quite enough!' Sheba shouted, pulling him away and shoving him behind her skirts.

'Ah, Sheba. Delightful to see you again.'

Peeking around the open door, Inji could see a young, well-dressed man, standing by the fireplace. He had sun-gold, wavy hair, oiled and brushed back from his face, hanging in curls to his collar. His skin was pale and smooth, his eyes a pure summer blue. His suit was silver grey, with an embroidered scarlet waistcoat and cravat. Clothes that looked like they cost more than the house they were standing in. Everything about him was pristine and perfect, including his warm, welcoming smile. Even his teeth looked like something from an oil painting.

Standing beside him was, at first glance, another suited man. But when Inji peered closer, she could see it was actually a lady. She wore trousers, leather gloves, a frock coat, cravat and shirt – all coal black – and her raven hair hung loose about her shoulders. In contrast, her skin was ice white, her dark eyes ringed with kohl, looking like holes punched in snow.

Why is she wearing a suit? Inji thought, before remembering her own choice of outfit. That might have made her warm to the unconventional stranger, if it hadn't been for that stare she had. She looked like she might butcher everyone in the room, just for a spot of morning exercise.

'Lucas,' said Sheba, smiling back at him. 'What a lovely surprise.'

'Forgive me.' Garrow bent to take Sheba's hand and lightly kissed the back of it. 'But we were passing by, and I had a package to deliver. I should really have informed you I was coming.'

'Not at all,' Sheba said. 'We are so pleased to see you.'

Garrow smiled again, teeth sparkling. 'And this . . .' he gestured to the suited lady, 'is my father's new servant, Macha. She has been ordered to follow me everywhere, each time I leave the house. It's most tiresome. And please forgive her . . . *unusual* . . . taste in clothes.'

Macha bowed, her eyes never leaving Sheba's. Inji noticed trinkets in her hair: black feathers, hidden among the tresses. Rook or raven probably. *Come to think of it,* Inji wondered, *she does have more than a whiff of bird about her.*

'Pleased to meet you,' said Sheba. 'We have some introductions of our own. This is Inji, and Pyewacket will go and fetch Glyph and Sil . . . won't you?'

Inji stepped into the room and did something between a curtsy and a bow. Who knew how you were supposed to act around posh people and their scary servants? At the same time, Sheba shoved Pyewacket out into the corridor.

'Just you wait,' he called over his shoulder. 'You'll never believe what our Glyph can do!'

'Ah,' said Garrow, turning his sapphire-bright gaze to Inji. 'Children! How lovely. And are they . . . ?'

'Like us?' Sheba laid a protective hand on

Inji's shoulder. 'Yes. They are … Gifted. Like Pyewacket and me.'

'How fascinating,' said Garrow. 'You have started an orphanage! Macha is also like you fellows. Under those gloves, she has the talons of a raven. Show them, Macha!'

The black-clad woman scowled, and for a minute Inji thought she might step forward and punch Garrow, lord's son or not, but instead she used one gloved hand to pull the other free. The tips of her fingers were covered in ash-grey, leathery skin and tipped with curved black claws, sharp enough to prick out your eye.

She flexed them at Inji and Sheba, defying them to make a comment.

So that's *why she smells of bird*, Inji thought. She looked closer at the woman's hair and saw that the black feathers weren't an ornament. They were actually growing from her head, merging with the human hair above.

'That's interesting,' said Sheba, a frown creasing her brow. 'I thought your father didn't approve of people who weren't *normal*.' The word came out with just the touch of a snarl.

'Ah!' Garrow blushed crimson and flapped his

hands about as if he didn't know what to do with them. 'Ha! Well, um, I believe he isn't *completely* against them . . . it's just . . . erm . . . um . . .'

'He thinks it's fine for them to be his servants,' Inji finished the sentence for him. 'But not to be friends with his son.'

A silence fell across the room, thick enough to cut with a knife. Sheba stared at Garrow, Garrow stared at Inji and Macha bit back a smile, a twinkle in her dark, rookish eye.

'Here they are,' said Pyewacket, barrelling into the room and shattering the awkward moment. 'Sil here looks like an armadillo and a rhino had a baby, but Glyph has a talent that will blow your pantaloons off!'

'Really?' Garrow stared at the two boys, a look of sudden interest on his face. *He's getting his own private sideshow*, Inji thought. It made her want to grab Sil and drag him out of the room, away from these strangers' eyes.

Pyewacket was hopping from foot to foot. 'Yes, write down a number. Any number. The bigger the better!'

'Macha?' Garrow said. His servant shot him a glare, her head twitching like a jackdaw's, but still reached a gloved hand inside her jacket to bring out a notebook and pencil.

'How many digits?' she said. When she spoke, her voice had a thick Irish accent. *Dublin or Cork*, Inji thought. She'd known lots of Irish immigrants in her time on the streets. The poor parts of London were full of them, fleeing from the famines in their home country.

'Four!' Pyewacket shouted. 'No, five. Six!'

Macha tutted and her pencil scratched away. She looked up when she'd finished, head tilted to one side like a raven considering which of your eyes to peck out.

'Don't show us! Don't show us!' Pyewacket led Glyph into the centre of the parlour. 'Now, then. Watch this. Do your thing, little mate!'

Glyph nodded and sat cross-legged on the floor. He drew his battered deck of cards from his pocket and shuffled them quickly, throwing in a couple of flips and turns. Then he stopped, stared at Macha for a moment, and dealt out six cards ... *fnap, fnap, fnap* ...

2-6-0-8-1-9

Macha blinked those night-black eyes two, three

times. Then she tore the sheet from her notebook and held it up. The same numbers were written there in scratchy pencil.

'How about that? Amazing, eh?' Pyewacket hooted and danced.

Inji looked at Garrow. He was gaping at the page in Macha's hand and the cards on the floor, mouth open.

'That's flummoxed you, hasn't it?' Pyewacket jeered. 'All your science and engineering gubbins can't explain *that*, can it? It's magical! It's a miracle!'

'I ... I ... I suppose so,' Garrow managed to say. 'It's incredible. Wherever did you find this child, Sheba?'

'That,' said Sheba, 'is a long story. Perhaps I could tell it while Pyewacket makes us some tea?'

'Yes. Tea. Lovely,' said Garrow. He sank into an armchair, still stunned. Pyewacket was sent off to make tea, Glyph and Sil tagging along behind him like shadows.

While they were gone, Sheba began her tale of the Hunters' Club, reminding him of the sensational crimes, and then all they had discovered since the rescue of Inji, Sil and Glyph from the packing crate. Garrow listened intently, while Macha stood at his side. She spent most of the time glaring at Inji, who had taken a similar position next to Sheba. Inji glared back.

Cat beats bird, she thought. *Give me any trouble and I'll claw the feathers out of your head.* She also began to wonder why Lucas Garrow needed a bodyguard. Was he too scared to go out on his own? Or was it because his father didn't trust him? Perhaps she was there to spy, just in case he went to visit Sheba against Daddy's wishes . . .

Pyewacket clattered back into the room with a tray of tea things, just as Sheba was finishing her story.

'So, you see,' she said. 'We're really at a loss for what to do now. We've exhausted all our leads, and I can't think where to look next.'

'That is a shame,' said Garrow. He rubbed his manicured fingers over his chin. 'I would dearly like to see these fiends stopped. For the sake of all London's more . . . *unusual* citizens.'

Macha leaned over to whisper in his ear. Garrow nodded up at her.

'That's a splendid idea, Macha. Why don't you share it with everyone?'

Macha gave a grunt before she began to speak. For

a servant, she didn't seem very keen on taking orders. 'What about trapping them?' she said. 'Lure them out. Then gut them.' She flexed her gloved hands and Inji saw the tips of her talons poke through the leather, hungry to rake and tear. Inji supposed the Hunters' Club were a threat to her too.

'That's not a bad idea,' said Garrow. 'You know this other sideshow owner, yes? And she must still have some kind of contact with these villains?'

'She swore she didn't,' said Sheba. 'Although I wouldn't trust her word.'

'You would be wise not to. She must have made good money from selling her acts. She would definitely take the opportunity to do so again. I would wager anything that she knows how to get in touch with them. Your leads are far from exhausted, Sheba: you now have knowledge of someone who can bring the Hunters' Club straight to you.'

'And what would we use for bait?' Inji asked, knowing full well what Garrow's suggestion would be.

He gave a sigh before answering. 'I'm afraid that would have to be one of you. A brave soul to draw them out, and perhaps lay a trail for the others to follow. These cads are clearly desperate to capture folk such as yourselves. There would have to be a convincing prize for them to bite at.'

'And what would the trail be?' Pyewacket asked. 'Breadcrumbs? That didn't work out so well in the fairy tale, did it?'

Garrow smiled. 'Perhaps I might have a suggestion. The reason for my visit was to deliver a gift. Now I see the gift itself might be perfect for the task ahead. It's almost as if it were fate!'

He held a hand out to Macha, who reached into the pocket of her black frock coat and drew out a slim, rectangular box of dark wood. She handed it to Garrow, gingerly, as if it contained something dangerous.

'Pyewacket, my friend,' said Garrow. 'I have been inspired by your Putrid Poo Projectiles, and have devised a treat for you in my workshop.'

'A present? For me?' Pyewacket's yellow eyes rolled and his mouth stretched into an excited smile. He clutched his hands together, beaming.

'Yes.' Garrow opened the box to reveal twelve grape-sized glass balls, resting on the velvet lining. 'These are a new, more potent version of your missiles. I have distilled the essence of a range of foul-smelling items into a liquid and trapped it within these globes.

They should explode on impact when fired from your catapult, releasing an odour most noxious. I call them "stink bombs".'

Pyewacket took the box from Garrow's hand, tears of joy in his eyes. 'I . . . I don't know what to say! This is the best thing anyone's ever given me!'

'You're very welcome,' said Garrow. 'I thought they might serve as a new design for your business, but now I believe they may have another use. If *you* were to be the one captured by this club, you could use them to lay a trail. Sheba would easily be able to follow it with her keen sense of smell.'

'Lucas,' said Sheba. 'That's a brilliant idea.'

'Wait a minute!' The look of joy on Pyewacket's face faltered. 'Me? Captured? Why do I always have to be the bait? Why can't one of the nippers do it?'

'I don't mind,' said Inji, quickly. This was a chance to prove herself, to become a true part of the team. She *refused* to miss it.

'Oh no,' said Sheba. 'It would be too dangerous for the children.'

'I agree,' said Garrow. 'In fact, I would be happy to have them stay with me, once you have arranged the details.'

'With you?' Sheba looked shocked. 'No, no. That would be too much. They will be fine here. Inji will look after them, won't you?'

Inji glared. She wanted to be out on the mission, not staying at home like some kind of nanny.

'Or perhaps Macha could assist?' Garrow suggested. 'I'm sure she has a way with children.'

A way of eating them, Inji thought. There was no way on earth she was being left in a house with that bird-thing.

'You're too kind,' said Sheba. 'But that won't be needed. Once I have followed the trail to the Hunters' Club location and freed Pyewacket, we will hurry back. All that will be left to do is inform the police.'

Inji thought back to her own kidnapping experience, and the ordeal of Gobbleguts. 'But what if they knock Pyewacket out?' she said. 'That's what they did to all the others. If he's not conscious, he can't lay a trail.'

'Good thinking!' Sheba smiled at her. 'They used chloroform to capture Gobbleguts. Pyewacket will need a mask of some kind, to stop him breathing it in. He can slip it on, just before he's snatched . . .'

'Now wait a minute . . .' Pyewacket started to say,

when one of his new stink bombs rolled from its box to fall on the parlour rug. It bounced once, twice, then landed in the fireplace and cracked open with a *tink!*

There was a *whoosh* and a cloud of purple gas began to fill the room, followed by a stink like nothing Inji had ever imagined. She had smelt the sewage-choked Thames in high summer; she had inhaled the odour of seven-week-old dead dog; she had slept in a room with pure-pickers and their buckets of runny, coagulated plop.[x] All of those fragrances seemed like fresh roses in a spring breeze compared to what was now flooding the parlour. It burned her eyes, it seared her nostrils. The contents of her stomach began a sudden rush up towards her mouth.

'*Gak!*' Garrow clamped a hand over his mouth. 'I would suggest . . . an immediate evacuation!'

Coughing, choking and retching, they all fled the room, then the house, gathering on the pavement outside to gulp in lungfuls of sooty London air, as if it were the purest Swiss oxygen.

'How . . . how long does it last?' Sheba managed to say.

'Not too long.' Garrow mopped his eyes with a silk kerchief. 'I made it potent, but not lingering. Most of the stink should have escaped up the chimney within a few minutes. The only person who might notice it is you, Sheba. With that incredible sense of smell you possess.'

'It's . . . it's . . . *perfect*,' said Pyewacket. He clutched the wooden box to his chest and beamed. 'Please, sir, I want some more!'

'Certainly,' said Garrow, managing a sickly smile. 'I will send some over as soon as they are done. And I will want to hear all about your mission. Please do let me know if I can be of further assistance. Catching actual villains – how jolly exciting!'

With that, the gentleman and his father's servant climbed into the carriage that had been waiting for them on the pavement: a gleaming black thing with a coat of arms painted on the side. As they trotted off, Macha could be seen glaring from the window. Inji matched her stare, then turned and followed the others as they made their way, step by careful step, back into the house.

Babysit the boys? she said to herself. *You must be joking. I* am *going to get my claws on those hunters. I swear it on my nine lives.*

Somewhere, in the back of her head, the cat yowled.

Chapter Ten

In which Pyewacket and Inji return to the stage.

The next few days were spent working: Sheba on the breathing mask, Inji on Sheba. She stood beside the table as Sheba tinkered, bombarding her with convincing arguments.

'I *really* think I should be there. I know Pasternak, after all. And you can't trust Pyewacket to do anything properly. He'll be too busy thinking about setting up his first stink bomb shop, or some such nonsense.'

'That's true,' said Sheba, speaking around the screwdriver she was holding in her teeth.

'And there should be two of us, really, in case anything goes wrong with one of the masks. If Pyewacket can't lay a trail, you won't be able to follow him, and he'll end up getting shot.'

'I've considered that,' said Sheba. 'I shall ask the Gutter Brigade to keep a secret eye out. They can let me know which way the hunters have gone.'

'But they're only children too!' The unfairness made Inji almost shout. 'And they can't watch every street in London. The hunters could easily slip by.'

'True again,' said Sheba. She took the screwdriver from her mouth and pointed across the room with it. 'But who will look after the two boys? We can't all be there, it will ruin the trap.'

Inji followed Sheba's gesture. Sil and Glyph were in the workshop with them. Glyph was carefully inking some new pasteboard cards for his deck. Sil had discovered the giant map and had become instantly fascinated. He was tracing the networks of streets with his fingers, just like he used to trace the chimney smoke in the sky. Inji had taught him a few road names, and he muttered them under his breath, like a mantra.

'Rosemary Lane, Cable Street, Cannon Street,

Whitechapel Road . . .' It was the most she had ever heard him say in one go.

'They'll be fine on their own,' Inji said, trying to sound convincing. 'Glyph has looked after Sil lots of times. As long as I'm not gone too long, he won't be a bother.'

'But you might be away most of the night,' Sheba said. 'If the hunters take the bait, they will have to be tracked, and then I will have to mount some kind of rescue. It could take hours, and might be *very* dangerous.'

'All the more reason to have me there!' Inji popped the claws on her hands, held them up as evidence. 'You'll need me if there's a fight. How are you going to manage on your own?'

Sheba patted some items on the workbench next to her. A walking cane topped with a carved wolf's head, a leather-bound book and a cylindrical silver perfume bottle. Inji knew they would not be what they seemed, but couldn't imagine what secret uses they had been put to.

'Show me, then,' she said.

Sheba grinned, keen to demonstrate her inventions. She picked up the cane and slotted the book on to it, a few inches before the handle. Inji could now see the book was solid wood, painted to look like it had pages. The perfume bottle clipped to the cane in front of the book, then Sheba clicked a hidden catch somewhere. A trigger and hand grip popped out from the book, and aiming sights flicked up along the back of the cane. With the cane's head as a stock, the collection of items had become a rifle.

'Sniper's sharpshooter,' said Sheba. She opened one end of the silver bottle to reveal a ring of chambers, each loaded with one of her sleeping darts. 'Repeating mechanism. Six shots. I should be able to pick off the hunters at a distance.'

Inji sighed. 'Yes, I suppose that's useful. But I still think you need me there. And I *really* want to do it.' She couldn't say why, exactly. The thought of the Hunters' Club scared her, and she dreaded seeing Pasternak again, but those feelings were nothing compared to her urge to join Sheba. Was it hatred of the hunters? Perhaps. The need for revenge? Maybe. But most of all, she thought, it was because she wanted to show her worth. Because if Sheba needed her – *really* needed her – then she and Sil and Glyph might actually have a proper home for good.

Inji looked up to see Sheba staring at her intently. Those amber eyes, piercing through her, past the tough street-girl act, past the hissing alley cat, right to the heart within.

'You don't have to prove yourself to me, Inji,' she said. 'I already know you're brave. I know you're kind, I know you're a good person. I can see all that from the way you take care of the boys. Risking yourself won't make me think any more or less of you.'

'How did ... ?' Inji began, then had to stop because of the lump in her throat.

'How did I know that's what you were doing?' Sheba gave a sad smile. 'Because I was the same girl once. I took silly chances and pushed myself in ways I shouldn't, just because I thought it would make my new friends like or need me more. In the end, though, I discovered they liked me anyway. Just for who I was. And *then* I was able to start liking myself.'

Inji wiped her eyes with the back of her hand. How could someone know just what she was feeling so completely? It was like her head had been opened up, like it had been laid bare on a doctor's table ...

Sheba took Inji's hands in her own. She gently rubbed the fur on their backs and then gave them a soft squeeze. 'Very well,' she said. 'You can come. But only if you follow my orders to the *absolute* letter. No heroics. No risks. Not for my sake. And only if you're sure Sil and Glyph will be safe on their own.'

Inji let out a gasp that made Sil turn from the map to stare. She rushed around the workbench and hugged Sheba tight. 'Anything you say.' She spoke into Sheba's clothes. 'I promise. And . . . thank you.'

Sheba hugged her back, and then gently peeled her away. 'Well, then,' she said. 'I suppose I should set about making an extra mask.'

*

The following morning, they were all in the front parlour, running through the plan while Sheba made some adjustments to her mask design. A loud knock at the door made everyone jump.

'I wonder if that's Lucas again,' said Pyewacket, as Sheba took the prototype mask from his mouth and went to answer it. 'He did forget to give you a goodbye kiss when he was here last . . .'

Glaring at him, Sheba opened the door to find that he was nearly right. Lounging on the steps was the lean figure of Macha, still dressed in her crow-black suit.

'Macha!' Sheba couldn't hide the tone of cheerful surprise in her voice. 'Did you bring Lucas to see us?'

''Fraid not,' said Macha. Smiling, she pointed to the street beyond, where the shiny black Garrow family carriage was waiting, with its team of horses and cloaked driver. 'The boss wants a quick word wit' you. If it's not too much trouble.'

Inji felt a hiss building up in her throat as she watched the smug bird-woman tease poor Sheba. Along with the others, she moved to peer out of the front door, staring at the passenger in the carriage.

Instead of Lucas, a much older man could be seen through the vehicle's window. He was twice the size of his son, with a mess of thinning blond hair scraped across his head. Several chins and drooping jowls hung over his silk cravat, and deep-set grey eyes glared out of a ruddy face.

Sheba seemed to wilt at the sight of him. 'Won't

his lordship come in?' she asked.

'Doesn't want to,' Macha said, still with that smug smile. 'Can't think why. P'raps you could come down to speak wit' him?'

Don't do it! Inji wanted to shout, but Sheba was already on her way down the steps. Lord Garrow saw her coming and slid the window down.

'Good afternoon, your lordship,' said Sheba, giving a curtsy. Lord Garrow looked past her, to where Inji, Pyewacket and the others were poking their heads around the door frame.

'Are *those* your . . . children?' he asked, as if he were talking to a piece of dirt on his shoe.

Sheba looked back up at the doorway. 'They are in all but name,' she said. (Inji felt a quick buzz of pleasure zing up her spine.) 'We have taken them in, as they had no home.'

'Ah,' said the lord. Charity didn't seem to be an idea he was familiar with. 'My son tells me one of them has a parlour trick with numbers.'

'That's Glyph, here,' Pyewacket shouted down the steps, his chest puffed out with pride. 'He can tell you any set of numbers with his cards, he can. He can find the combination to any safe, any lockbox in the whole wor— Ouch!'

Inji cut him off by stamping hard on his foot. 'Don't go shouting that around!' she hissed at him. 'He's not a circus act, you know!'

'Can he indeed?' Lord Garrow stared at Glyph for a long moment before finally seeming to notice Sheba in front of him. His nose wrinkled as he looked down at her. 'I believe my son came to visit you again,' he said. 'Here. At this . . . *house.*'

'He did,' said Sheba, shooting a glare at Macha, who had obviously been snitching.

'Well, it shall be the very last time he does,' said the lord. 'I have forbidden him from having any further contact with you. And you shall not seek to communicate with him. I've heard all about your ridiculous plots and plans. *You*, madam, are a bad influence on him.'

Sheba seemed to be too shocked to speak, but Inji felt a white-hot ball of fury burn her insides. Claws popped, she began to head down the steps to Lord Garrow's carriage, but one of Sil's strong hands stopped her. Pyewacket and Glyph grabbed her too.

'Don't be stupid!' Pyewacket whispered in her ear. 'If you attack a lord, you'll spend the rest of your days in the deepest, darkest prison cell in England! And us with you!'

Inji struggled for a moment, but realised Pyewacket was right. Forcing herself to be still, she listened as Lord Garrow said his piece.

'If you think you can disobey me, I urge you to reconsider. I know several people who can make life very difficult for you. And your . . . *kind*.'

With that, he banged on the carriage roof, signalling the driver to crack his whip. Macha shoved past Sheba – a fraction too roughly – and climbed up on to the back of the vehicle. Then, with its wheels striking sparks from the cobbles, the horses pulled it away as fast as they could gallop.

Sheba stood silent for a moment, watching it go. When she turned to walk back, there were tears in her eyes.

Inji felt her stomach twist with sorrow for her new friend. But she had also heard Lord Garrow's words and they whirled around her head.

'He's a toff,' she whispered to Glyph. 'And he knows people who can hurt our "kind". Are you thinking what I'm thinking?'

Glyph reached into his coat pocket with two

fingers and drew out a card to show her. It was a freshly inked picture of a skull with fox ears and smoked-glass goggles.

*

A black cloud hung over the house for the rest of the day. It was even worse because they had to pay another visit to Madam Pasternak.

Sheba and Inji went together, late that afternoon. They marched straight through the bar of the Three Castles and into the back room, where they were surprised to see Pasternak packing up her things into a large carpet bag.

'Going somewhere?' Sheba asked.

At the sight of her, Pasternak shrieked, which brought Bruno and Gruno running from the back room. When they spotted Sheba, they shrieked too. Bruno, arm in a sling, turned around and leapt back through the door. Gruno stood there, his face a sickly shade of green, his bottom lip trembling.

'I told you the troof! I promise I did!' Pasternak wailed. 'I 'eard Gobbleguts was wiv the Scarlequins! That's the God's honest!'

'We're not here about that,' said Sheba. 'We have a proposition for you. To do with your show.'

'Show? What show?' Pasternak pointed to her bulging carpet bag. 'I'm packing up, ain't I? I only 'ad two freaks left, and they've both gone orf somewhere. Now I'm out of business.'

Sheba raised an eyebrow. If Pasternak expected any pity, she was talking to the wrong person. 'I want you to put on one more show,' she said. 'And I want you to contact the man with the red moustache. You must tell him you have two more acts available for purchase.'

'Jigger off,' said Pasternak, as bravely as she was able. 'I won't be doing nuffing for the likes of you. And I don't know anyfing about that ginger toff. Couldn't speak to 'im if I wanted to. Which I don't.'

Sheba's hand moved to the pocket of her peacoat, where the walnut handle of her dart pistol was peeping out. 'I don't believe you,' she said. 'I think you can contact him any time you like. And you *will* be putting on a show, or at least advertising one. I want him to capture Inji here, and my friend Pyewacket. And I want it all to look very convincing. If it doesn't . . .' Sheba let the edge of a growl creep into her voice, 'I will be very, *very* unhappy.'

'And,' Inji added, 'we'll be going to see the crushers. I'm sure they'd like to hear all about the evil baby farmer, hid away in a Cheapside tavern.'

Pasternak's pale face drained the very last drop of blood it held. 'You . . . you'd peach on me? You'd snitch on your old boss?'

'With pleasure,' said Inji. 'Baby farmers are even lower than sideshow owners in my book. The law's too. They'll string you up like a kipper.'

Pasternak looked to Gruno for help, but he was edging his way out of the room, his lip still jittering. She swallowed hard, then slumped her shoulders.

'All right. All right. I'll do it. But only if you promise to leave me alone. I never want to see either of your faces again after this.'

'That would be our pleasure,' said Sheba. She took a card from her bag and held it out for Pasternak to take. 'Send word here as soon as it's arranged.'

*

It was noon the next day when they heard, much quicker than anyone expected. Sheba was beginning her first meditation session with Inji in the upstairs room that had once been Sister Moon's. Inji was trying to concentrate, but there was a stuffed two-headed sheep in the corner that kept distracting her.

'Inji!' Sheba snapped. 'Stop staring at Flossy and concentrate! You have to *breathe.* Centre yourself on your breath.'

'I'm trying . . .' Inji began, when the bell for the front door rang. Pyewacket could be heard, stomping along the corridor to answer it.

'Ooh,' his voice floated up the stairs. 'If it isn't Gruno. Or Bruno? You two are so handsome, it's hard to tell you apart.'

Both Inji and Sheba made a dash for the stairs, clattering down together and sprinting to the door.

'Would you like to come in for a cup of tea?' Pyewacket was saying. 'Or I can fetch Miss Sheba to give you another kicking?'

Sheba yanked the door wide, and Inji peered through Pyewacket's legs. Outside on the step was the hulking form of Bruno, his arm still bound in a sling.

'Madam P sent me,' he said. He flinched from

Sheba's glare and took a step backwards into the street. 'She says she spoke to that geezer. He wants to see the new freaks before he pays for 'em. Says it has to be tomorrow night.'

'Tomorrow?' Sheba said. 'So soon?'

'Keen as mustard,' said Pyewacket. 'Can't we make it next week? Maybe next month? Next year, even?'

'Has to be tomorrow,' Bruno repeated. And then he practically sprinted away, down the street and out of sight.

'Look, I've changed my mind about all this,' Pyewacket said, as soon as the door was shut. 'There must be some other way to go about it. Or someone else to do it. What about moggy chops there? She's gagging to be the bait. Let her do it on her own.'

'She's just a child,' said Sheba. 'She shouldn't be doing it at all, really. And you've had experience of this sort of thing.'

'Oh yes!' Pyewacket's tusk-filled mouth curled in a grimace. 'Experience of nearly getting chomped by a giant metal crab! Experience of being pulled around on a bit of rope like a worm on a hook!'

'I don't mind doing it on my own,' said Inji. 'I'm not scared.'

'No,' said Sheba, arms folded. 'The masks are ready. The rifle's ready. You've even got your new stink bombs to use, Pye. The plan goes ahead. Tomorrow night.'

'If it wasn't for the bombs, I wouldn't be doing it,' Pyewacket muttered, as he slunk off down the hall.

Inji and Sheba went back to their meditating, but if it was hard to focus before, it was impossible now.

Tomorrow night, Inji kept thinking. *It's happening tomorrow night.*

*

Funny, Inji thought. *You move away from somewhere, spend months or years doing different things, being a different person . . . and then you go back and it's like you never left. Like all that time in between was just a dream.*

She was standing behind a sheet of stained tarpaulin in the back room of the Three Castles. On the other side of that thin sheet were fifty drunken boozers, all shouting at the tops of their voices.

Every now and then came the *smash* of a dropped glass or the sound of someone being sick.

'Nervous?' Pyewacket asked. He was standing next to her, dressed in a cloak and a wizard's hat painted with arcane symbols. His face had gone a strange shade of green.

'Not really,' said Inji. 'I did this every night for months. In fact, this crowd seem quite tame compared to usual.' She peeped through a hole in the tarpaulin. There was a sea of grubby, beetrooty faces, and the stink of unwashed bodies and sour gin. Somewhere among all that was Sheba, dressed in jacket and trousers, with her hair tucked under a sailor's cap. And somewhere else was the man with the red moustache, waiting to drag them off to the Hunters' Club.

'I'm about to soil my undercrackers,' said Pyewacket. He wrung his big, spidery hands together, fingers slithering over one another like spaghetti. 'In fact, I think I might have already.'

'Why are you scared?' Inji asked. 'You used to do this all the time, didn't you?'

'That was years ago,' said Pyewacket. 'What if I've lost my edge? What if I'm not entertaining enough? And besides, back then there weren't cold-blooded killers in the audience, waiting to snaffle me.'

'Relax,' said Inji. 'This lot don't want to hear anything you say. They want to laugh at the way you look. All you need to do is jump around a bit, show them your long arms. Pull a few funny faces. Then dodge the glasses they throw and get off the stage. After that, we just have to let whoever comes for us think they've knocked us out. Have you got your mask ready?'

Pyewacket reached into his pocket and held up a small cup-like device. It was just the right size to fit over his nose and mouth, and had a rubber seal around the edge to stop any gas seeping in. Inji patted her own pocket, where an identical one was hidden. Pyewacket nodded and gulped.

'You know,' he said, 'you're all right, really. I know I tease you a bit – I can't help it. Cruel words just pop into my head and then, before I know it, I've said them.'

'Thanks,' said Inji. 'The same thing happens to me. You need a sharp tongue when the whole world is always against you.'

‘Well, *we’re* not.’ Pyewacket gave her a nervous smile. ‘Me and Sheba, I mean. You’re one of us.’

To her surprise, Inji felt the urge to cry. To disguise it, she peeked around the edge of the tarpaulin. Madam Pasternak was taking to the stage, flanked by Bruno and Gruno. Somewhere in the corner, Winston had wheeled in a battered old piano and was trying to play a tune on it.

‘Laydeez and gentlemen!’ Pasternak shouted for the third time. ‘Laydeez and gentlemen!’ And then, with a bellow that would have put an army sergeant to shame: ‘OI!! YOU BUNCH OF DRIBBLING, GIN-SOAKED HALFWITS!! STOP SHOUTING AND LISTEN!!’

The noise of the crowd instantly stopped, all eyes turning to the stage.

‘That’s better,’ said Pasternak. ‘And now, for your entertainment, may I present the latest addition to Madam Pasternak’s Circus of the Bizarre: the mysterious, the magical … Wyepacket the witch’s imp!’

‘She’s even got my flipping name wrong,’ muttered Pyewacket. He shook his head and stepped out on to the stage.

There was stunned silence for a moment, then the whole place erupted in yells and jeers.

'Look at the size of 'is arms!'

'Are they real?'

''Ave a butcher's at 'is face![xi] It's like a box of smashed kippers!'

Inji watched as Pyewacket spread his arms for quiet. When that was ignored, he did a couple of backflips and stood on his hands. One or two cheers could be heard among the screaming.

'Now that I have your attention,' Pyewacket shouted. 'Prepare to be mystified as I reveal the dark arts of my mistress: the witch of Bodmin Moor! Gasp in horror as I predict the future, using my incredible powers!'

He cleared his throat and placed one hand on his chest, the other outstretched, as if he was about to deliver a speech from a Shakespeare play.

''Twas a dark and stormy night, two hundred years or more ago. A storm was raging across the windswept moor when, all of a sudden . . .'

Several empty bottles flew from the crowd, forcing Pyewacket to dive to the floor. They smashed on the wall behind him, soaking him with beer.

'That blooming nearly hit me, you savages!' he yelled. Madam Pasternak hastily stomped on to the stage and shoved Pyewacket back behind the tarpaulin.

'The magical Wyepacket!' she bellowed. One person near the back gave a half-hearted clap. 'And now, the return of an old favourite. One half of the Gargoyle Family, the child whose mother was attacked by a tiger while giving birth: it's the fearsome Cat Creature!'

'I would say "break a leg",' Pyewacket whispered to her, 'except you probably will if they hit you with one of those bottles.'

Inji winked at him, then stepped out on to the stage. More screams and insults, but it was nothing new to her. She dropped on all fours, baring her teeth, and gave the loudest hiss she could muster. The front row of the crowd jumped back, out of her way, knocking people over behind them.

Bottles and glasses came flying, but Inji was already on the move. She'd taken off her boots to set her clawed feet free, and as she leapt to the wall, she used them to dig into the woodwork, hanging there like a spider.

Another bottle swished its way towards her head, leaving a trail of beer like a comet. She was off before it hit, pushing hard to leap across the room and hang upside down from one of the rafters.

'Here, pussy, pussy! Here, cat!' screamed one of the punters. Inji felt a sudden rush of anger . . . she hadn't had to face such insults for a while and her skin had grown soft. But instead of reining it back, she allowed her cat self to hiss and spit as much as it liked. She felt her teeth grow sharper, her claws sink deeper. As her eyes shrank into slits, the darkness of the room seemed to ebb away. Now she could see the faces of the mob below her. There was Sheba – cap pulled down, cane in hand – looking up at her with sad eyes. Around her were ugly, dirty, toothless faces, roaring and laughing. And there . . . could that be Redtash? A man stood silently watching her: he had broad shoulders and a woollen cap. Heavy black coat with the collar turned up.

She didn't have time to stare too long. More bottles swished up towards the ceiling and she jumped, leaving them to smash and spray the crowd with watery beer and broken glass.

'The terrifying Cat Creature!' Pasternak was

shouting, over the cries of the soaked audience. She quickly ushered Inji off the stage before a riot erupted. 'And now I shall entertain you with a selection of popular ballads!'

There were boos and wails, which suddenly stopped as soon as Bruno and Gruno stepped up to flank their mistress. Inji didn't notice. She was too busy panting and shaking, trying to bring her cat-ness back under control.

'Blimey, look at you!' Pyewacket said, pointing at her. She raised her paws . . . no, *hands* . . . to touch her face. There was more fur there than usual, all bristled and electric, and her ears had tweaked into sharp points.

'I'll be . . . back to normal . . . in a minute.' She managed to squeeze the words out without hissing. Before she could completely control herself, the tarpaulin twitched aside. Two men stepped in, pulling the cover back behind them.

'Excuse me,' one said in a posh, public-school drawl. 'We have an appointment with Madam Pasternak.'

The speaker wore a sailor's coat with a peaked cap on his head. He had a long, narrow face with sharp cheekbones and deep-set eyes. But next to him was someone else . . . someone she both dreaded and wanted to meet at the same time. It was the man in the black coat and cap from the crowd. Except now she could see him properly: his hooked nose, his cruel eyes, the bandages that covered Sheba's angry scratches on his neck . . . and his red moustache.

Chapter Eleven

In which things go horribly wrong.

Inji froze.

All those thoughts of revenge and bravery, all that urgency to be face to face with Redtash, right in the middle of the action . . . vanished. Her limbs locked, her brain shut down. All she could think was: *it's him.*

'Madam Pasternak?' said the shorter man again.

It was Pyewacket who came to his senses first. He nodded at the pair of strangers and jerked his thumb over his shoulder. 'She's just on stage, performing,' he said. 'If you can call it that.'

'Perhaps you could get her attention for us?' When Redtash finally spoke, his voice had the same accent as his friend's. And Inji recognised it perfectly from the night she was kidnapped at Skinker's.

'Certainly, guv'nor.' Pyewacket gave Inji a nudge, nodding his head towards the stage. *This is it*, Inji thought. *This is when we get snatched. Stop staring at that bloke and* do *something.*

She shook her head to clear it, and then copied Pyewacket, turning towards the stage, her back to Redtash and his friend. As she moved, her left hand dipped into her pocket and brought the mask up, pressing it over her nose and mouth.

She had a view of the stage, of Pasternak screeching out a tune that sounded like a peacock being strangled, and then she *sensed* a movement behind her. Glancing sideways at Pyewacket, she realised – with horror – that he wasn't wearing his mask. The fool had forgotten to put it on.

Inji reached out to nudge him, to warn him, but it was too late. Strong arms came from the shadows behind, wrapping her in a crushing grip. A hand was clamped over her nose and mouth, pressed hard against her face. Even with the mask on, she could smell a whiff of strong chemicals, enough to make her head spin. She remembered Sheba's words: *struggle for a few seconds, then let yourself relax. Pretend you're asleep: limp and lifeless. Don't make a sound or movement until you're sure they're not watching.*

Hoping and praying she was convincing, she kicked and squirmed for the count of ten, then went as floppy as a rag doll. From the corner of her eye she saw Pyewacket do the same, except *he* wasn't pretending.

And then she was up in the air, flung over a shoulder. Her head faced the ground and all she could see was stained floorboards and puddles of beer. The man holding her marched out through the back room and into the alley behind the pub. Inji could smell horses, hear their quiet whickering, and all the time her mind was racing. *Pyewacket is* really *knocked out! And he's got the stink bombs! What if they put us in different crates? Or in different carriages? How will I lay a trail? How will Sheba find us?*

With a grunt from her captor, she was heaved in the air and slung into a box. Then the lid slammed shut and everything went dark.

*

'Pyewacket?' Inji whispered, as softly as she could. 'Pyewacket?'

He was in the crate with her. It was too dark to see, but she could feel the softness of his body next to her, and hear him snoring through his fanged mouth.

They were beginning to move along the streets. The cart juddered and lurched over cobbles, rocking her from side to side.

'Pyewacket!' she whispered again, and nudged him in the back. All she got was more snores. It sounded like he would be asleep for quite some time.

The cart bumped again. Every heartbeat took them further away from the pub, further away from Sheba. Would she be out there, following them? Or would she still be in the crowd, listening to Pasternak screeching? After all, they had been snatched and taken out the back. With the tarpaulin blocking them from view, Sheba might not even know anything had happened.

There was only one thing she could do. Inji had to start laying the trail herself. *Now.*

She reached across and began to pat Pyewacket's pockets, searching for the wooden box with the stink bombs in. Her mind raced with visions of Sheba trying to find a trace of them and failing. Of them being hunted by the men in animal masks. Of dying alone in a moonlit wood.

Please be here, please be here, she mouthed. Nothing. She reached over to Pyewacket's left side and began to pat, finally feeling something box-shaped in his inside pocket.

Breathing a sigh of relief, Inji slid it out. She opened the lid and ran her fingers over the marble-like bombs inside. *Eleven.* Now she had to find a way of dropping them for Sheba to follow.

She looked around for the knothole that she'd peered out from before.

It was gone.

Stupid, she told herself. *This isn't the same crate. That one was left on a cart in the middle of Hackney Road somewhere.*

But if there was no knothole, how was she supposed to drop the stink bombs? Claw one out? That would take ages, and besides, the hunters would hear it.

Think, Inji. Think. Might she be able to lift the crate lid? She thought back to the moment she had been dumped inside. She'd been worried about taking her mask off and hiding it in her hand. Had she heard them nail the lid on?

No, there hadn't been time. They must have been in a rush to get away.

In that case . . . She reached up and pushed against the top of the crate. It budged a smidgen. *Quietly, now. Oh so quietly* . . . Inji pushed a bit harder, using both her hands. The lid moved slowly upwards. If the wood squeaked, though . . . If one of the hunters looked round . . .

When there was a gap of a few inches, Inji wedged her fingers in. With her other hand, she opened the walnut box and drew out a stink bomb. She waited until she felt the cart bump over another pothole and she flicked it out of the gap. There was a moment's silence and then . . . had there been the tiny *tinkle* of glass breaking, or had she imagined it?

Oh, please, let it have worked.

There were ten bombs left now. North London was about, what . . . four or five miles away? If she dropped one every half mile she wouldn't run out. But would the trail be strong enough for Sheba to follow?

There was only one way to find out.

With her eye squeezed to the chink in the lid, Inji

began counting the horses' hoofbeats, trying to keep track of the distance. Half her mind kept thinking back to that first kidnapping, when the urchins of the Gutter Brigade had run along beside the cart. She looked for them now but, if they were around, they were keeping well out of sight.

We're on our own, Inji said to the cat in her head. There was nothing she could do but count the distance. And pray.

*

Through the gap under the crate lid, Inji watched London changing. As they moved further north, the houses began to shrink. There were fewer and fewer people on the streets. One or two trees appeared, then a hedge. Soon they were travelling on a dirt road, past cottages and fields. Inji had never seen so many plants and bushes. And the air . . . she could breathe in lungfuls of it without having to cough or retch.

But this wasn't a weekend excursion into the countryside. She was being driven to her execution. That is, if Sheba wasn't out there somewhere, coming to the rescue.

With trembling fingers, Inji flicked out the second-to-last bomb. It bounced on the edge of the cart, then disappeared into the darkness. There were no street lights out here, and if it wasn't for her night vision, she wouldn't have been able to see anything but smudges.

She began to count the horses' hoofbeats again, ready to drop the final piece of her trail. She had estimated that five hundred might make up half a mile. But that had just been a panicked guess. *Mother, if you're up there, watching all this, please let me be right.*

As if in answer, the cart turned off the road, and Inji heard the crunch of gravel under its wheels. They had arrived at the hunters' house.

*

Inji lay back in the crate, stuffing the last stink bomb in her pocket. She tried to look as unconscious as possible, even though her heart was hammering against the bones of her ribcage and every ounce of cat-ness in her body was telling her to run for her life as soon as the crate was opened.

There was a squeak of wood and a rush of cool air. Hands hooked under her armpits and she was scooped up from the crate, slung over a shoulder. She smelt more of that fresh, clean goodness; trees, grass, earth.

'Why do I have to carry the ugly one?' Redtash was speaking. 'He's heavy as an elephant.'

'Because you're so big, strong and dashing,' said the one carrying Inji. The men started walking, talking as they went.

'The one you've got,' said Redtash. 'It's definitely the girl from the other night. That Skinker fellow sold her to me, along with two others.'

'Stupid creature must have run back to the nearest sideshow. Although I suppose her kind don't know any better. Too dumb to do anything else, what?'

'These things probably have brains the size of peanuts. But I do wonder why Gwydion wanted a hunt tonight. The moon isn't full. And that cat thing is feisty. She'll be a challenge.'

'I expect he was in a rush to test out the new crossbows.' The man carrying Inji stopped. There was the sound of a door being unlocked. 'They arrived today. Fresh from his factory. I haven't even unpacked them yet. He must be eager to try them out on some living targets.'

'They're here?' Redtash sounded excited. 'Show me!'

'In a moment. Let's get these two safely locked away first.'

They moved inside the house. Inji heard feet on floorboards and smelt furniture polish and varnish. She chanced a peek to the side and saw she was in a grand building, with tall windows looking out on to a long driveway, flanked with trees.

They moved through one, two rooms, and then they were going down some steps. Gas lamps hissed on the walls, and the air became cooler, damper. *A cellar*, she thought, remembering Gobbleguts's story.

There was a clang of metal, and then she felt herself being heaved up and over. She fell through the air, landing on a hard stone floor. A second later, Pyewacket flopped beside her. The cage lid banged shut, a lock clicked, and she heard the footsteps of the two hunters going back up the steps, leaving them alone. And trapped.

*

'Pyewacket, *wake up*!' Inji shook him again. This time he began to stir. She gave him another dig in the ribs, just to make sure.

'Ow! What did you do that for?' He blinked his yellow eyes, and then covered them with his hands. 'Owww, my head! I think I'm going to be sick . . .'

Inji wiggled as far away as she could, back against the bars of the cage. She watched Pyewacket's face turn purple, then slowly fade back to a pallid, blotchy pink.

'You forgot to put your mask on, you great plum,' she hissed. 'You've been asleep the whole way here.'

'Here? Where's here?' Pyewacket rubbed his eyes and looked around. He put a hand out and touched the iron bars of the cage.

'We're in the cellar of the Hunters' Club,' said Inji. 'The one Gobbleguts told us about. Don't worry, though. They're going to let us out in a minute.'

'Are they?' Pyewacket gave a sigh of relief. 'That's nice of them.'

'Yes,' Inji hissed. 'They're going to let us out and then *shoot* us!'

'What are you angry with me for? I said this was a bad idea, right from the start. Now there's no trail, and Sheba will never find us!' Pyewacket looked like he was about to cry.

'*I* laid the trail,' said Inji. She held out the last stink bomb for him. 'I took these out of your pocket and dropped them on the way. There's one left. Do you think Sheba would have been able to track us? Will she be able to rescue us?'

Pyewacket took the stink bomb and turned it over in his fingers, frowning. 'I don't know,' he said. 'I was hoping she would spring us as soon as she knew where their house was. Something must have gone wrong. Did she see us get taken?'

'I don't know,' said Inji. 'It all happened so fast. We were behind the tarpaulin and they went straight out the back door. If she was in the crowd, she might not have noticed.'

'Princess Beatrice's bottom burps!' Pyewacket cursed. He rapped himself on the head with his knuckles. 'Come on, Pye. Think. *Think.* What would Sheba do?'

Inji thought too. Their best bet was to get out of there now, before the hunters came back with their new crossbows. She stood up, as much as she was able, and tried to get a look at how the cage was shut.

'Padlock,' she told Pyewacket. 'A big one. Can you pick locks?'

Pyewacket shook his head. 'Sheba could. She'd have us out of this thing before you could say *Dickens' dog did a doo doo in the dairy.*'

'Well, she's not here, is she? Can you use that stink bomb? Stun them when they come down to fetch us? Then we can put on our masks and dash through it. It might give us a head start.'

'I could try,' he said. 'But if there's any open ground outside the house, we'd be sitting ducks.'

Inji thought of that long gravel driveway. There was a good fifty yards to cross before they even made it to the trees. The hunters would be able to pick them off like fish in a barrel.

'I'm going to scratch their eyes out!' She could feel her anger making the cat in her head bristle. 'I'll take at least one of them before they get me!'

'No.' Pyewacket reached up and took both of her hands. He pulled her down, so they were sitting face to face. 'Inji. Listen. I know I lark about all the time . . . but this is me being serious. *Deadly* serious.'

'Pyewacket, you're scaring me.'

'Scaring *you*? I'm terrified. But this is what we

have to do.' He breathed in deeply. 'We let them take us out. We let them lead us to wherever they want to hunt us. If Gobbleguts's story was true, they'll give us a head start. I want you to run as fast as you can. Use all that cat power you have. Head for the city and run, run, run.

'Then you find Sheba, and you tell her where these toffee-nosed bludgers live. You tell her to get all the police in the city and bring them back here and nab them.'

'What about you?' Inji's voice shook. 'What are you going to do?'

'Me?' Pyewacket tried to laugh, but it came out as more of a sob. 'I'm going to draw them off. I'll create a diversion, so that you can get away.'

'No!' Inji squeezed his hands. 'Don't do that! We can get away together! Or we can hold them off until Sheba gets here!'

Pyewacket shook his head. 'Won't work,' he said. 'We'll both end up dead. At least this way, one of us survives. At least we have a chance to stop them.'

'You'll be killed!' Tears began to spill down Inji's furry cheeks. 'They'll shoot you!'

Pyewacket was about to answer, when a laugh

echoed around the cellar. It was joined by another, and another. They spun round to see four of the hunters, all dressed in their leather jackets and animal masks: a fox, a tiger, a panther and a lynx.

'Of course we're going to shoot you!' the fox said. His face was hidden behind the mask and goggles, but Inji recognised Redtash's voice. 'Have you seen these beauties? They're amazing!'

He held up the crossbow he was holding, showing it off. It looked lean and new and deadly. Fresh oil gleamed on the wooden stock and the steel bow. A rectangular box jutted out underneath it, and Inji could see a black-feathered bolt already fitted. The point looked barbed and hungry.

'You won't get away with this!' Inji's scream was raw and desperate, with the edge of a cat's hiss to it.

'Quiet, you disgusting beast!' Redtash aimed the crossbow at her, his finger on the trigger. There was a *click* as he pulled it, and then a *whoosh* as the bolt flew out. At the last second, he shifted his aim, so that the bolt cracked into the stonework above the cage. It stood there, juddering, as the hunters laughed again.

'Now watch *this*,' said Redtash. He gripped a

handle on the side of the bow and pulled it back. There was a *clunk* as the string recocked itself and a fresh bolt shot up from the box below to take the first one's place. 'Self-loading. Gwydion has excelled himself. These things are a work of genius!'

'Where is he?' The second man who snatched them spoke. 'Does he not want to help us test them?'

'He can't make it any more,' the hunter with the panther mask said. 'He sent a message to my club earlier. Some excuse about business in the city.'

'Never mind,' said Redtash. 'He'll just have to miss out. Let's get on with it, while there's still a bit of moonlight.'

Redtash produced a key and unlocked the cage. He swung the lid up, all the while keeping his crossbow aimed at Inji's head. 'Don't try anything, wildcat,' he said. It sounded like he might be smiling under his mask.

The other hunters moved to grab Inji and Pyewacket. They twisted their arms back and held them tight, so there was no chance of escape. With Redtash taking the lead, they were forced up the stairs and through the house, out on to the driveway.

Inji saw nothing but trees all around. No lights,

no houses. Nobody to hear them if they screamed for help. She looked up to see clouds scudding across the night sky, cloaking everything in gloom. *At least that's some advantage*, she thought. *And they probably don't know I can see in the dark.*

She used that sense now, scanning every bush and tree around the estate. Her eyes flicked from shadow to shadow, desperate to see the outline of a body, or the glint of starlight on a makeshift sniper's rifle.

Sheba, she thought, over and over. *Sheba, where are you?*

But there was no sign of any other living soul besides her, Pyewacket and the hunters. Sheba wasn't here.

The plan had failed and they were all on their own.

Chapter Twelve

In which Inji and Pyewacket become prey.

Inji and Pyewacket were shoved, struggling, across the drive to the trees at the side of the house. Both of them fought back, digging their heels in, kicking up sprays of gravel. But the hunters were much stronger. They bent Inji's arms until she felt like they were going to be ripped off. She had no choice but to go where they directed her.

They passed manicured bushes and statues of angels, looking beautiful and serene in the moonlight. It wasn't right, them looking so peaceful, Inji thought. *Not when Pyewacket and I are about to get murdered.*

She thought of Sil, trying to hold his image in her

head. His soft brown eyes, the feel of his knobbly hand in hers. Was she really never going to see him again? How would he cope? Who would look after him?

And then they were in among the trees.

This part of the grounds was wild and rooty. There were huge oaks and elms, with clumps of fern and bramble growing in between. Inji's bare feet sank into the spongy loam of dead leaves. She felt twigs and acorn shells between her toes. Unlike the trimmed and clipped neatness of the house's gardens, this was what the land had once truly looked like. The kind of place the real Wild Hunt might have galloped through, horns blaring, hounds baying, chasing down their prey.

Inji looked up through the branches at the sky. There was a waning moon, but it kept drifting behind those banks of cloud, plunging the woodland into even deeper darkness.

Good, Inji thought. *Keep on doing that. The darker the better.*

When they reached a clearing, the hunters stopped, releasing their prisoners. They formed a circle around them, crossbows at the ready. Inji rubbed at her sore shoulders and stared at the tips of those arrows, imagining them plunging into her flesh, cracking her bones like twigs.

'Welcome to our club,' said the tiger-masked one. 'I doubt you'll enjoy the membership as much as we will.' There were laughs from the others.

'Allow me to explain the rules,' said Redtash. 'We will give you a ten-minute head start. Then the hunt will begin. If you manage to escape . . . well, there's no point in telling you. Because you *won't*.'

More laughter, until Inji couldn't stand it any longer.

'Why are you people doing this?' she cried. 'What gives you the right to hunt and kill us? Do you hate us that much, just because we're different?'

'You're an abomination,' said the hunter with lynx ears. 'God made man in his own image – it says so in the Bible – and anything that spoils that image should be wiped off the earth.'

'The Bible doesn't have pictures though, does it?' Pyewacket said. 'For all you know, Adam and Eve could have had purple skin and elephant trunks. And tails.'

'I've never read the Bible,' said Inji. 'But I know

it says in there that you shouldn't kill. We might not look the same as you, but we're still human beings.'

'Forget the Bible,' said tiger-mask. 'People have been killing each other over that book for centuries. It's just an excuse. Jamik here hates you because you're different, and different makes people scared. Personally, I couldn't care less what you look like. I just love the thrill of chasing you through the woods and ending your pathetic lives.

'So, if you don't mind, I have a gentlemen's club breakfast to attend in the morning and I would rather like to be getting on with things. Your head start begins . . . *now.*'

Pyewacket stared at her. Inji stared back. Then he reached over, grabbed her hand and ran.

*

They sprinted as fast as they could, crashing through the undergrowth, thorns tearing at their clothes and skin. They leapt over roots, bounced off tree trunks, ducked under brambles.

Finally, when they stumbled into another clearing, they stopped.

There were thick woods all around. Impossible to know which direction they were even facing. *Maybe if I knew how to read the stars . . .* Inji thought. She looked up, noticing the overlapping stripes of branches, criss-crossing each other against the clouds. She felt an instinct then – a deep memory that was part of the cat in her.

Trees. Climbing. Safety.

Of course! Why hadn't she thought of it earlier? But then she had never really climbed a tree before. Rooftops, walls and fences, definitely . . . but trees, the ones that were in the heart of London, were mostly stunted, poisoned things, their trunks covered with carvings and playbills.

'Right . . .' Inji managed to speak, in between panting for breath. 'This is good . . . we might have a chance . . .'

'A chance? Are you crazy?' Pyewacket looked back the way they had come. In a few minutes the hunters would be following, crossbows firing.

Inji pointed to the trees. 'They don't know how good we are at climbing, do they? I'm faster than you, but still . . . the pair of us are more at home up *there* than down here. They've brought us to the best place possible.'

'Genius!' Pyewacket slapped her on the back. 'You're a fur-faced genius! I should have made you my business partner when I had the chance.'

There still is a chance, Inji felt like saying. But then she realised there might not be. A lump of fear and sadness closed up her throat, and she had to bite her lip to stop herself wailing.

'Now get going,' Pyewacket said, his face becoming deadly serious. 'Climb and run. Remember what I said . . . Fetch Sheba. I'll draw them off.'

Inji shook her head. She tried to clutch at him, but he was already moving – bounding up the nearest tree trunk in quick, loping leaps. 'Pyewacket! No!'

'Do it!' he shouted. 'Do it now!'

And then he was off, swinging arm over arm through the trees, heading eastward into the thickest part of the wood.

Inji watched him go for a second before realising that standing still was a *really* stupid thing to do. She headed for a tree as well and leapt, sinking her claws into the bark as she landed.

Five quick jumps and she was up among the top

branches. Trees were *much* easier to grip on to than walls. And there were pathways everywhere: lines of wood and leaf leading off in all directions.

For a few seconds she dithered, wondering whether to follow Pyewacket. But what good could she do? Away to the south was London, and Sheba. And the police. If she moved as quick as lightning, would she get there in time to bring them back and save her friend?

You'll never know if you sit here thinking about it, her cat voice said.

'You're right,' Inji whispered. She jumped for the nearest branch and started to bound along it, faster than she had ever moved before.

*

Leaping from tree to tree soon became as natural as walking.

Inji's feet were still bare from her performance at Madam Pasternak's, and she used all four sets of claws to stay firmly anchored to the branches. It wasn't long before she reached the edge of the woodland. Scampering up to the highest reaches of a tall beech tree, she paused to scan her surroundings.

Beneath her was the shady darkness of the woods. Her night vision cut through it like butter, showing her the paths in between the trees.

Nothing moving. The hunters wouldn't even know she was here. She'd left no tracks, no broken twigs or scuffed moss. There was no sign of her for them to follow. Even if they knew she'd taken to the trees, they wouldn't be able to see her. Not with those stupid smoked-glass goggles they all wore. The autumn leaves were starting to turn red and gold, but hadn't begun to fall yet. They hid her from sight completely, especially in the murky darkness.

'Thank you, clouds,' she whispered. They were still sweeping across the sky, keeping everything nice and gloomy.

She turned her attention away from the woods: south, towards London.

A stream ran alongside the edge of the trees, opening out into a reed-lined lake in the distance. Inji guessed that must be the place Gobbleguts had blundered into and hid.

Beyond that was a series of hills, mostly covered by fields and copses. Here and there was a house, and further out were clusters of lights that might be villages. On the horizon was a bulging bank of smoke that glowed orange from within. Here and there it was pierced by a spire or steeple. *London*, Inji thought. It looked a long way away, especially for a girl with no boots on her feet.

Do I go now, she wondered. *Or do I wait for daylight?*

The longer she took, the less chance Pyewacket had of surviving. If he had any chance at all.

Inji turned back to the woods. She peered down into the darkness, willing her slitted pupils to open as wide as they could. She pricked her ears, which had tweaked themselves to points, and strained every sense, trying to catch some sign of Pyewacket.

She heard woodland rustles. Creaking branches, scampering creatures. She could smell bark and earth and moss.

'Where are you, Pye?' she whispered. 'Don't say they've got you already . . .'

Her head was filled with visions of him, peppered like a pincushion with those black-feathered bolts. Hanging lifeless from a tree, pinned to the trunk, blood pattering on the leaves below . . .

'Damn it, Pyewacket. *Damn it.*'

There was no way she could leave him. Even though he'd told her to. Even if Sheba never found them. *Even if it meant never seeing Sil again.* She wouldn't be able to live with herself, knowing she might have saved him but didn't.

'I don't know what good I'll be,' she whispered to the darkness and the trees. 'But I'm coming.'

Stupid, stupid, stupid, said the cat in her head, as she turned away from London and began to leap from branch to branch, back towards the hunters.

Shut up, Inji told it. *It'll be fine. We've got nine lives, haven't we?*

Haven't we?

It didn't answer.

*

The woods, it turned out, were quite big.

Inji travelled quickly, keeping as high as she could, using the leaves for cover. She went all the way back to the clearing they had run from. She could see the roof of the manor house, the path they had been dragged along, and tracks spidering off in all directions. All of them empty – no sign of Pyewacket.

And then, off to the right somewhere, a voice:

'Coo-ee! Has anyone seen a bunch of posh dunderheads, dressed up as puppies and kittens? Has anyone told you how stupid you all look? I've just met a fox who says he wants his ears back!'

Then came a chorus of *twangs* and *thuds*.

'Missed me! You lot couldn't hit an elephant's backside with those things. Call yourself hunters? You should change your name to the Short-sighted Ratbags' Club!'

Inji turned to face Pyewacket's voice and started making her way towards him. Slowly, this time. There were sure to be hunters around.

'Jamik! Go to the left and flank him! He's in the treetops somewhere.' She heard Redtash below. Close by, but still hidden in the shadows. Holding her breath, Inji began to creep down the trunk of a tree, head first, eyes scanning the darkness.

'Why didn't anybody check if he could climb?' Another voice echoed through the wood. It sounded like the tiger-masked one.

'How were we to know? Just because he has arms

like a gibbon, we didn't think he'd be able to move like one.'

There was a crunch of feet on leaves. Inji froze.

She saw two shadows moving between the trees: Redtash and tiger-mask heading deeper into the woods. She was about to follow when she sensed another presence. There, by that oak: another hunter. The one with the panther mask. He was leaning against the trunk with his crossbow trained on the treetops. If it hadn't been for her night vision, she would never have seen him.

Now what do I do? Coming to the rescue had seemed right a few minutes ago. But how was a small girl supposed to overpower a grown killer, armed with a deadly crossbow?

Scratch. Tear. Bite. Her cat instincts were buzzing with adrenaline, ready to fight to the death. Her human side, though . . . that knew better. The hunter had his finger on the trigger, and he was much bigger and stronger than her. Whatever she did, she had to be clever.

But what should *I do? Leap on his head? Try and hit him with a stick?* Her only chance was to knock him out quickly. Then maybe she could take his crossbow, use it against the others. *Except you've never fired one before in your life. And it probably weighs a ton.*

While she was racking her brains for a plan, she heard more shouts in the distance. This time it sounded like Pyewacket was in trouble.

'Aaargh! My arm! You shot me in the arm, you great stinker!'

Come on, catgirl, Inji thought. *You have to do something* now.

She tensed the muscles in her legs, ready to spring from her tree trunk, using her speed and weight to hit panther-mask in the head.

But then, just as she was about to leap, he clapped a hand to his neck and grunted. Then he dropped his crossbow and crumpled to the floor.

What? Inji flicked her eyes between the trees. Had someone shot him? Was there somebody else in the woods?

A slender silhouette separated itself from the shadow of a beech tree. It stepped on to the path and walked closer, stopping when it was directly below Inji.

'You can come down from there now,' it said. 'I

might need your help.'

Sheba! Sheba had come! Inji leapt down from the tree and into her arms.

*

'How did you find us?' Inji whispered, even though she felt like whooping. 'Where were you? We were so frightened!'

Sheba put a finger to her lips. 'Hush,' she whispered back. 'I'll explain later. We have to help Pyewacket.'

Inji could see that Sheba was still wearing her disguise from Pasternak's audience. Her wolfish eyes glowed orange beneath the peak of her cap and she clutched the long-barrelled cane-rifle in her hands. She reached into her pocket and pulled out her clockwork pistol, handing it to Inji.

'In case you need it,' she whispered.

Inji clutched it to her heart and, with padding feet, they both began stalking the remaining hunters.

*

They came across the first one a few moments later. The man with the tufted lynx ears poking up above his goggles. Inji saw him flitting between the trees and grabbed Sheba's shoulder. Sheba's amber eyes blazed as Inji pointed him out, and she lifted her rifle to aim.

She sighted down the barrel and pulled the trigger. There was a soft *ping!* The hunter staggered sideways and collapsed against a tree.

Inji held up two fingers for Sheba to see. *Two more.* She nodded.

*

'Come down! We will bandage your arm for you!'

Inji and Sheba heard Redtash calling long before they saw him. They moved quickly and silently towards his voice.

'I don't believe you!' Pyewacket called out. 'You'll skewer me with arrows as soon as I poke my head out!'

As if in answer, there was a *twang* from somewhere among the trees, followed by the sound of an arrow thudding into solid wood.

'See! I told you! And you missed me again! Why don't you take those stupid goggles off? You can't shoot for toffee!'

'He's right,' said the tiger-masked man. 'These goggles don't help your aim unless the moon is full. We'd be better off . . .'

His sentence remained unfinished as he tumbled to the floor, his crossbow clattering out of his hands. Sheba had shot him in the neck from twenty paces away. Redtash whirled round, his bow up and ready.

'Who goes there?' he shouted. 'Drop your weapon or I'll shoot!'

Safely hidden in the shadows, Sheba took aim again with her rifle. Inji watched her finger close on the trigger. There was a muffled click, and then a strange *sproing* sound.

'Blast it,' Sheba hissed. 'The mechanism's jammed!'

'What do we do now?' Inji whispered.

'We charge him,' Sheba replied. 'Try and get a shot in with the pistol. It only works at close range. After he shoots, we'll have a few seconds while he reloads.'

Inji nodded. She looked down at the weapon in her trembling hands.

'Ready?' Sheba whispered. 'Now!'

They dashed out from behind the tree at the same time, one on each side. Redtash spotted them and fired his bow. The bolt was a streak of silver in the gloom – Inji could see it coming and kept low, feeling the wind on her cheek as it whistled past, thudding into a tree somewhere behind her.

Redtash was already grabbing the handle and cocking his bow for another shot. As fast as they were sprinting, they were still nowhere near him.

'Shoot!' Sheba yelled, and threw her rifle at the hunter. Inji saw it go sailing, end over end. She raised her pistol and squeezed the trigger, sending a dart flying. It hit the leather of Redtash's jacket with a soft *pop*, just as Sheba's rifle clattered into his head.

The shock from both impacts made him stagger, but his bow was still in his hands and now ready to fire. A low growl came from his throat, making him sound as much an animal as his attackers.

'You go high!' Sheba shouted, as they sprinted the last few steps. In slow motion, Inji watched Redtash's bow swing towards Sheba, just as she dropped to skid along the woodland floor, kicking up a cloud of leaves behind her. Inji gave a yowl and *pushed* with her powerful catlike legs, leaping up at the hunter's head. She sailed through the air, claws jutting as far as they would go, and hit him full in the face with her body. She dug in with hands and feet, feeling her talons sink through the fox fur of Redtash's mask, into the skin beneath.

'Aaaargh!' he screamed, as the impact of Inji and Sheba knocked him off his feet. His bolt zinged off into the woods somewhere and he crashed backwards into a tree. A moment later, in a frenzy of flailing arms and legs, they were all on the floor. Redtash was screaming and trying to pull Inji off his head, but her claws were sunk deep into her prey. She wasn't going anywhere.

'Hold him,' said Sheba. Inji looked across to see her reaching up under her hat, bringing out a hairpin with a jewelled head. She jabbed it hard into Redtash's leg and pressed the end with her thumb. 'Anaesthetic,' she said. 'He'll be out in a second.'

Sure enough, the hunter soon stopped struggling. His body went limp and his hands dropped away. Inji figured it was safe to let his head go. She pulled her claws free, wincing as she realised how deep they had sunk.

'What's going on?' A familiar voice came from somewhere above them. 'Why haven't I been shot yet? Inji? Why are you still here? And who's that with you?'

Pyewacket's terrified face appeared through a clump of leaves, like a nightmare version of the Cheshire Cat. He stared for a moment, and then his jaw dropped open.

'Sheba? Is that you? You could have got here a bit earlier! Perhaps just before we both nearly died!'

Lying among the twigs and leaves, amazed and delighted to still be alive, all Inji could do was laugh.

*

It took them the best part of an hour to drag all four hunters out of the woods and manhandle them on to the cart. In between all the heaving and cursing, Sheba told them what had happened to her.

'I saw the two men go behind the tarpaulin,' she said, 'and I guessed they were going to snatch you. Only I couldn't get close enough to see. The crowd was pushing and pulling … most of them were trying to escape out of the door, to get away from

Madam Pasternak's singing.

'Anyway, by the time I got there, you were gone. I went through the back door and saw the alleyway empty. There were tracks in the dirt: horses' hooves and cart wheels, so I guessed you'd been loaded into a crate. Then I tried to follow the scent.'

'Wasn't it easy to track?' said Pyewacket. 'The way those bombs stink … I'm surprised half of London wasn't running away, screaming.'

'They're strong,' said Sheba, 'but they seem to fade into the air quickly. Especially outside. Within a few minutes they had mingled with all the other London stenches. There was only a ghost of a trail to follow. I had to go back and forth several times to make sure I was on the right track. Luckily the Gutter Brigade were on the case. Snatcher had seen you leave, then Scribbles and her sister Bimsy put me back on the trail. I wouldn't have found you without them.'

'We thought you weren't coming,' said Inji. She was surprised to find tears pricking her eyes. She had felt so helpless, so terrified …

'I'm sorry,' said Sheba. 'I really am. When the buildings and houses thinned out, the trail was easier to follow. I ran as fast as I could, but by the time I found the house, you had already been taken inside. The cart was here, and the crate. I found the empty box the stink bombs had been kept in . . .

'And then the other hunters arrived in their carriages. I dashed into the trees and waited. I knew they would bring you out at some point, and I made myself ready. I wish I'd had some way to let you know . . .'

'Don't you *ever* moan at me for being late again,' said Pyewacket, sticking his tongue out.

Inji laughed and cried at the same time. She wrapped her arms around Pyewacket and squeezed. 'You were so *brave*,' she said. 'You were going to sacrifice yourself for *me*.'

'Yes, well.' Pyewacket blushed. 'It was all a bit dramatic, wasn't it? Let's not mention it again. Although the blighters did nearly take my arm off . . .'

He pointed to his elbow, where there was a bloodstained tear in his shirt. Sheba inspected it. 'It's just a scratch,' she said. She tore a strip from her own shirt to bandage it.

'It jolly well nearly severed an artery,' said

Pyewacket, wincing. 'I'm lucky to be alive, you know.'

Inji clambered up on to the cart and looked at its cargo of sleeping hunters. With their eyes hidden, it was impossible to tell whether they were alive or dead. On impulse, she reached down and pulled their goggles and face masks off. With just their animal ears remaining, they all looked more ridiculous than scary.

'What are we going to do with these?' she said.

Sheba climbed up to stand beside her. 'Ah,' she said. 'I *do* recognise them. The tiger is Lord Roebuck, and the panther Lord Beecher. The lynx is Beecher's younger brother, I think, and the other . . . our friend with the red moustache . . . I recall being introduced to him by Lucas. Fleetwood, his name was. He was the son of a disgraced nobleman. That explains why he's been running around doing the dirty work for the others. Trying to get back into society's good books, I imagine.'

'A bunch of lords and gentlemen,' said Pyewacket. 'There's no way this lot will be going to prison. Their posh families will have all this swept under the carpet, you mark my words.'

'I've been thinking about that,' said Sheba. 'And I've had a few words with Large 'Arry down at Pickle Herring Wharf. You remember him, don't you? He was friends with Mama Rat.'

'What are we going to do, put them on a slow boat to China?' Pyewacket asked.

'Better than that. One of 'Arry's sons is first mate on the *Hougoumont* – a ship that take convicts to Australia. He's kept a spot free on the next boat out. One of the deepest, darkest cells in the hold that they keep for the most dangerous inmates. These fellows are going to wake up and find themselves on a one-way trip to the other side of the world.'

'But what if they say they're gentlemen?' Inji asked. 'Won't they just be released?' Even a young street child like her had a good grasp of the way justice in Great Britain worked.

'Who's going to believe them?' Sheba grinned, showing her sharp canines. 'Half of the convicts on the ship are probably saying the same thing. No, we won't be seeing this murderous scum for a long, long time.'

'Well, we'd best get them down to the docks, then. Before they wake up,' Pyewacket said. 'But I'm keeping a crossbow as a souvenir. If I can work out how it's made, it can be my next business venture. Ten times more deadly than Poo Projectiles.' He picked one up and aimed around the grounds with it.

'I'm not sure those things should go on sale,' said Sheba. 'They could be very dangerous in the wrong hands.'

Looking at the weapon again reminded Inji of something. 'What about "Gwydion"? He's not here. That means one of the hunters is still at large.'

'Yes!' Pyewacket hopped up and down. 'He's the one that built these bows! Oh, I'd love to get my hands on him too!'

'Perhaps there's a clue on the bow,' said Sheba.

'Like a maker's mark?' Inji pointed to what her sharp eyes had spotted on the stock. There was a name, burnt into the wood.

'*Fenric & Co.*,' Pyewacket read.

'Is that the place by the Leather Market in Bermondsey? With the stone wolf on the roof?' Inji and Sil had climbed up there many times, pretending to ride on the wolf's back or curling up between its legs to shelter from the rain.

Sheba nodded. 'Perhaps we should pay them

a visit,' she said. 'They will have records of who ordered weapons to be made. Or perhaps this Gwydion even owns the factory, if he's as rich as his other friends. But that can wait until tomorrow. I've had enough excitement for one night.'

Inji yawned, suddenly feeling tired to her bones. She curled up on the driver's seat as Pyewacket took the reins and let the rocking motion of the cart soothe her as they headed out on to the track, back towards the smoggy streets of London.

*

The church clocks were striking three in the morning by the time they got home. They had left the horse and cart with Large 'Arry, as payment for adding four new prisoners to his son's cargo. Inji's bare feet were sore as they scuffed over the dirt and cobbles, but she was too tired to care. All she could think about was cuddling up next to Sil in their pile of blankets and sleeping, sleeping, *sleeping*.

Pyewacket was first up the steps. He pulled a door key from his pocket and then turned back to look at them, his face horrified.

'Sheba,' he whispered. 'Something's wrong. The door . . . it's been broken open.'

'What?' Sheba moved to look, but Inji was already racing up the steps, pushing past her.

'Sil!' she cried. 'Silas!' She hurried through the door and into the house, calling out her brother's name. Nothing answered her but echoes.

She ran into the parlour – it was empty – and then pounded down the hall to the kitchen, where she could see a gas lamp had been left on. She could hear the others following her, but all she could think of was her brother. *Please be in here! Please be safe!*

Skidding into the kitchen, she saw at once that her every worst fear had come true. There were broken chairs and shredded blankets all around the room. Smashed plates and cups littered the floor; the table had been roughly shoved into a corner. Some of Glyph's cards still lay on top of it.

But of Glyph and her brother, there was no sign.

They had been taken.

Chapter Thirteen

In which the Carnival comes to the rescue.

Inji stood in the middle of the kitchen, hands clasped to her head. She couldn't think, she couldn't breathe. It was like a giant, invisible fist was squeezing her body tighter and tighter, pulping her lungs, crushing her stomach. She wanted to scream, but all that came out of her mouth was a low hissing sound.

'I don't understand . . .' Pyewacket was saying. 'We got the Hunters' Club. We got them. Who could have done this?'

'Everyone stay calm,' said Sheba. 'We need to keep a clear head. We need to look . . .'

'Gwydion,' Inji managed to say, even though her jaw was clenched hard enough to crack her teeth. 'We didn't get Gwydion.'

Pyewacket still held the crossbow in his hands. He looked down at the maker's mark, burnt into the wooden stock. 'Could it be him? Is that why he wasn't at the house? Was he trying to catch the rest of us too?'

'Don't jump to conclusions,' said Sheba. 'There's no way he could have known about us. And why would he want more victims when they already had you two?'

'What about Lord Garrow?' Inji shouted. 'He hates our kind. He must be the last hunter. And he saw us all. He knew Sil and Glyph were here!'

'You have no proof of that!' Sheba looked shocked. 'You can't accuse someone of kidnapping, just because he doesn't like us.'

'The factory, then. We have to go there. It's our only lead.' Inji began to move out of the kitchen, back to the street. Sheba blocked her way, taking her by the arms, oh so gently.

'Inji, wait . . .'

'We have to go!' Inji screamed, making the others flinch. 'We have to go *now*! They've got my brother!

Don't you understand?'

'I do,' said Sheba. 'I do understand. But we can't be sure that's where he is. Even if it *was* Gwydion who took him, they might have gone somewhere else. His townhouse, a country manor like Lord Roebuck's, a secret hideaway somewhere . . . If we run off to the factory without being sure, we could be making a mistake. We could be wasting valuable time . . . time that we need to rescue Sil and Glyph.'

Inji nodded. Her eyes blurred with tears, and every muscle in her body wanted to race out of Paradise Street, to find a trace of Sil, to do *something* . . . but she managed to keep herself still. Sheba was right. She trusted her, but . . .

'Pyewacket,' said Sheba, taking charge. 'Check the yard, the alley, everywhere. Look for tracks. Try and see which direction they went in.'

'Righto,' said Pyewacket. He ran past them, out through the back door.

'Inji. Look around. Is there anything that seems out of place? Anything that might give us a clue who did this?'

Inji scrubbed her eyes with her sleeve. She started to scan the room. Beside her, Sheba was doing the same, her nostrils flaring as she sniffed for a scent.

'There's nothing,' said Inji. 'Just broken stuff. Sil must have fought whoever it was. He must have . . .' she choked back a sob, 'and Glyph too. It looks like he threw his cards. Some fell on the table.'

'There's a faint smell . . . familiar, but I can't place it. Could Glyph have left a message for us?' Sheba walked across and flipped one of the cards over. It was a C. She turned over the others. N, E, F, I and R.

'Wait.' Inji rushed to the table and slid the cards into a different order. She stared down at the word she'd made, a ball of rage beginning to build inside her.

F-E-N-R-I-C

At that moment, Pyewacket came dashing into the kitchen. 'Cart tracks,' he said. 'But I can't tell which way they went, once they got on to the cobbles.'

'It doesn't matter,' said Inji. 'Glyph left us a message.'

'Get some weapons,' said Sheba. 'We're going.'

'To the factory?' Pyewacket asked.

Sheba pointed at the word on the table. 'To the factory.'

*

Of all the foul-smelling places in London, the Leather Market in Bermondsey stank the most. Which was really quite an achievement. Goat and sheep hides, stale blood and, worst of all, the gallons and gallons of dogs' mess used for tanning. The deadly mixture of awful scents tinted the thick smog yellow. It seeped into the bricks and stone of the buildings. The whole place reeked like a demon's underpants.

By the time Inji had sprinted all the way there, she was panting for breath. Gasping the poison air made her feel sick. She wrapped her shawl around her mouth, blinking her eyes against the fumes.

There, on the next street, was the Fenric factory. She could see the stone wolf silhouetted against the slowly brightening sky.

Sheba and Pyewacket were right behind her, feet pounding as they tried to keep up. Sheba was holding a parasol and had a leather satchel slung over her shoulder. Pyewacket was still carrying the crossbow. They had had to dodge several policemen on the way, who would probably have wanted to ask him a few questions about it.

'It's there,' said Inji, while the others caught their breath.

'What's the plan?' Pyewacket said, wheezing. 'Do we lure them out? Or sneak round the back? Maybe go in through the roof?'

'Who cares?' Inji snapped, and then she was off again, pelting around the corner. All she could think about was getting to Sil, even if it meant tearing through another of the hunters first.

As the factory came into view, she could see that it was all closed up for the night. The big workshop doors were firmly shut. There was a smaller door beside them, which must have been for the offices. Inji made for that and began yanking the handle.

'Let me try.' Sheba was close behind her, already reaching for her lockpicks. Nudging Inji out of the way, she knelt down and began tinkering with the lock. Seconds later, it clicked open, but the door still wouldn't budge.

'They must have barred it from the other side,' said Pyewacket. 'Shall we try the roof?'

'How will Sheba get up?' Inji asked. Sheba just smiled and waggled her parasol. It was made of white, lacy fabric with a wooden handle carved into a bird's head, but Inji knew it wouldn't be as useless as it seemed.

'Come on,' said Pyewacket. He shoved the crossbow handle through his belt, and then kicked off from the wall. His talon-tipped fingers grabbed the top of the door frame, using it to boost himself up to a windowsill, then a sign board. In a few leaps, he had slipped over the edge of the roof.

Inji followed, using her claws to scale the brickwork. She made the highest window easily enough, but the leap from there to the roof was a bit far for her. Her fingers scrabbled on the roof edge until Pyewacket's hand reached over and grabbed her.

'Thanks,' she said, as he pulled her on to the rooftop. They both looked down at Sheba on the pavement below. She had made her way across until she was beneath a winch that jutted out near the top of the wall. She pointed the handle of her cane at it and then, with a *thwip* sound, fired it upwards. The handle shot out, trailing a length of cord, and wrapped itself around the winch. Sheba gave it a tug and started to clamber up the building side.

A few minutes later, the Carnival were all

standing on the factory roof, looking out over a sea of gently smoking chimney stacks. Inji thought back to when this rooftop world had been a sanctuary for her and Sil. The wolf statue nearby still had their initials carved on it from when they used to sit beneath its legs, munching on a stolen apple or a bag of roasted chestnuts.

Now her brother was trapped somewhere inside – hurt, possibly. Maybe worse.

'There's a hatch,' said Pyewacket. 'Just behind the stone wolf.' He jammed his long fingers under the edge and heaved. 'Locked.'

Sheba rummaged in her satchel, bringing out a glass bottle of smelling salts. 'Stand back,' she said.

Kneeling at the hatch, she uncorked the bottle and poured the salts around the latch and hinges in a long line. Then she drew a red-tipped match from her jacket and flicked the end with her thumbnail. It flared into life with a sputter, before Sheba dropped it on the salts and stepped quickly backwards.

KRAKK!

There was an explosion like a firework going off. A bright flare that left glowing patterns dancing across Inji's eyeballs. The hatch splintered into pieces and tumbled back into the factory, leaving a gaping hole.

'Stay back! We're armed!' a voice called up from the gap, followed by the crack of a gunshot. The bullet hit the frame and gouged out a chunk of wood.

'So are we!' Pyewacket shouted. He pointed his crossbow at the hatchway and fired blind. There was a scream from somewhere inside.

'My foot! You've shot my chuntering foot!'

Drawing her clockwork pistol from her satchel, Sheba ran up to the smoking hole in the roof and dropped straight in, vanishing from sight in a second. Inji followed, grabbing the hatch edge with her claws and using it to swing herself into the factory, hoping there was some kind of platform beneath, and not a sheer drop to the workshop floor.

Luckily for both of them, they were above a mezzanine deck. To the right it dropped off into the open space of the factory floor: steam hammers, forges and workbenches, all dark and cold and sleeping now. To the left were the offices, behind a row of glass windows. Gaslights were on inside, illuminating the decking and the three men standing on it.

One was bent double, clutching his foot and screaming. Another was trying to hit Sheba with some kind of truncheon. Except she was busy dodging and twirling, getting in just the right position to bring the butt of her pistol up into her attacker's nose.

The third man was staring up at the ball of claws and fury that had just come swooping in from the roof.

Inji saw all this in one blink, before she reached the height of her swing and released her claws from the hatch frame. She let herself sail through the air, heading straight for the third man's face. Her feet hit him like a cannonball and he toppled backwards, cracking through the mezzanine railing and disappearing over the edge. Inji caught a brief glimpse of his flailing arms, then heard a *crunch* as he hit the workshop floor. There was a groan, followed by silence.

She landed herself, thumping down on her bottom a few inches from the decking edge. Looking round, she saw Sheba finish off her attacker with an elbow to the face and a knockout dart in his thigh. He slumped to the ground, sliding down the staircase behind him like a sack of potatoes.

Pyewacket had dropped through as well, and he clumped the screaming man with the butt of his crossbow, so hard that the stock snapped in half. His yells stopped instantly, and he fell to the deck in an unconscious heap. Pyewacket tossed the ruined bow on top of him. Then all three jumped up, ready to face more enemies . . . but the factory was silent. Deserted.

Except for the office. Someone inside gave a quiet moan.

'Sil!' Inji ran through the door, finding herself in the manager's room. A noticeboard with a map of London filled the far wall, with a desk in front of it. A stove crackled and smoked in the corner and there, tied to a chair with a gag in his mouth, was Sil.

'*Mmph!*' His scared eyes widened even further when he saw Inji, and he struggled against the ropes holding him down. Inji dived on him, wrapping him in the fiercest hug. She pulled the gag from his mouth, while Sheba drew a pocketknife and set to work on his bonds.

'Oh, Sil, Sil!' Inji hugged him over and over, kissing away the tears that spilled from his eyes. 'It's all right. I'm here now. Did they hurt you? Are you injured?'

She grabbed his hands and arms, checked them this side and that for cuts or bruises. But it would have taken a lot to get through the thick, bony plates that covered Sil's body. Apart from the shock, he seemed to be unharmed.

It was only after several minutes of fussing that his sobs ebbed away and Inji realised someone was still missing.

'Glyph! Sil, where's Glyph? Did they take him?'

Sil nodded. His eyes flicked around the room and low, miserable noises came from his mouth. All this drama, all this change, had deeply disturbed him.

'Can you tell us where?' Inji pressed. 'Did the people who took you say anything?'

Sil's gaze fixed on the large map above the desk. He reached out a hand to it.

'Now's not the time for maps, little mate,' said Pyewacket. 'We need to find Glyph as quickly as we can.'

'No.' Inji saw Sil was looking at the map in a different way. There was purpose in his eyes, beyond his usual trancelike fascination. 'Let him touch the map. I think he's trying to tell us something.'

Together they helped Sil out of the chair and

supported him as he clambered on to the desk. His bumpy fingers stroked the smooth paper of the map and began to trace the lines printed on it.

'Snow's Fields, Weston Street, Maze Pond,' he muttered. 'New Way, St Thomas Street.'

His fingers traced the roads from the Leather Market, heading north towards London Bridge and the Thames. Then they stopped. He stabbed a finger on to a spot and looked at Inji, as fierce as she'd ever seen him.

Inji peered at the place he was pointing to. 'Guy's Hospital,' she said. 'Did they take Glyph to the hospital, Sil?'

Sil nodded.

'Sil must have heard them talking,' said Inji. 'But why would they take Glyph there? Did they hurt him, do you think? Did he need a doctor?' Just mentioning it made her stomach twist.

'I think it might involve *this* gentleman.' Sheba held up a blue cardboard file that had been lying on the desk. A sepia-tinted photograph was pinned to the front. It was a hunched man with a great bald dome of a head and a pinched, wrinkled face. He looked like a goblin from a fairy tale.

'Sir William Jenner,' Inji read from the front of the file. 'Do you think *he's* Gwydion?'

'I doubt it,' said Sheba. 'He's quite famous. Queen Victoria's own doctor, no less. I can't see *him* using a factory in Bermondsey to make crossbows.'

'But what can Gwydion want with him? And why does he need Glyph?'

Sheba stuffed the file into her satchel and slung it over her shoulder. There was a grim look on her face, and her eyes had begun to glow a deep, furious orange. 'That,' she said, 'is what we are about to find out.'

They lifted Sil down from the desk and headed out of the office, down the stairs and back into the streets.

As they slammed the factory door shut, they failed to notice a single black feather that had got stuck in the frame. It fluttered up into the stinking air, then drifted slowly down on to the cobbles behind them.

Chapter Fourteen

In which there is a showdown at the hospital.

Every muscle in Inji's body burned like molten iron. The soles of her bare feet were numb and blistered, the bones of her heels beaten and bruised. And yet, somehow, she found the strength to run a bit more.

Pulling Sil by the hand, she followed Sheba and Pyewacket as they moved northwards through the streets, heading for Guy's Hospital.

Thankfully it was close, and within five minutes they had reached the front. A grand building, with a wing on either side, it was shaped like a giant horseshoe. In the middle was a large courtyard, and a stone wall with high iron railings blocked off the front. Set into that were wide metal gates, flanked by stocky pillars. Peering through the bars, Inji could see the rows of darkened windows. Inside, the patients would be sleeping, healing. Unaware of the drama going on just a few feet away from them.

'Gate's open,' said Pyewacket. 'Looks like our boy came in this way.'

One of the gates stood ajar, the lock broken.

'Could that be his carriage?' Inji pointed across the road to where a lightweight black hansom cab waited. A powerful grey stallion stood in the traces, tossing its head. There was no driver to be seen.

'Must be,' said Sheba. She slunk across the road to it, then ducked underneath. Inji saw the gleam of her pocketknife blade against the harness, and then the horse stepped free. Sheba reappeared and gave it a smack on the rump, sending it trotting down the road.

'Old Gwydders won't be galloping away now,' said Pyewacket, grinning.

'Either that, or there's a cab driver in one of these houses who's going to be *very* annoyed when he finds his horse gone,' said Sheba, as she returned. 'Come on, let's get into the hospital.'

Easing the gate wider, they slipped inside.

'We should go carefully,' Sheba whispered. 'There will be nightwatchmen about. Doctors and nurses too. We mustn't get caught or raise an alarm. We want to surprise Gwydion before he can do anything to Glyph.'

'How will we know where to go?' Inji asked. She looked around at the windows. There were three storeys of them on all sides. 'There must be hundreds of rooms. Which one is Jenner's office?'

'I'm betting it's that one,' said Pyewacket, pointing. One of the windows in the west wing, two floors up, had a light dancing through the glass. Not a gentle nurse's lamp, but a bright burglar's one, gleaming to and fro as the room was searched within.

'Somebody hasn't remembered they should shutter their lamp when they're robbing,' muttered Inji, then blushed as the others looked at her. She'd forgotten they didn't know much about her time with Skinker, when she was basically a thief.

'That's it! A robbery!' Sheba said. 'That's why he needs Glyph – to give him the combination for a safe. Gwydion must be stealing something from Jenner.'

Pyewacket frowned. 'But how does he know Glyph could do that? Or where to nab him from?'

'Lord Garrow knows about it. *You* were the one who told him, remember?' Inji glared at Pyewacket. 'Isn't that proof enough it's him?'

Sheba didn't say anything. She was rubbing her chin, thinking aloud. 'I wonder what he could possibly have in his office? All his gold and jewels would be in a bank vault or a house uptown, wouldn't they?'

'Who cares what it is?' said Inji. 'I just want Glyph back! Come on. There's a window open below. If we can get in there, we can sneak up the stairs and rescue him.'

Keeping low, they dashed across the courtyard until they were up against the west wing. With a final look around for guards, Pyewacket scooted up the wall and on to the ledge, Sheba's parasol clutched in his teeth. Inji followed him. The chiselled stone walls were harder to grip than the crumbling bricks she was used to, but her quick fingers found tiny gaps and ledges for her claws to catch on to. Soon, she was sitting next to Pyewacket on the sill.

'Gently does it,' he whispered, as he gripped

the bottom of the window. 'There's a ward full of patients on the other side.'

Peering through the sooty glass, Inji could make out rows of beds with sleeping bodies in. There was the sound of quiet snoring. Although, if they made any noise getting in, the snores would be replaced with screams. Waking up to see Pyewacket creeping into your room would not be the nicest of experiences. Like a shoemaker's elf from a horror story.

Pushing together, slowly as creeping snails, they inched the window open further until it was wide enough for them both to slip through. Then Pyewacket leaned back out and fired the parasol handle back down to Sheba. She tied the cord around Sil's waist, while Inji watched the room.

Please don't wake up, please don't wake up, she prayed. Pyewacket was beginning to grunt and strain as he tried to hold Sil's weight. One or two of the patients murmured in their sleep, making Inji's heart miss a beat.

'Let me help you,' she whispered, taking hold of the rope. Pulling together, they managed to heave Sil up and over the window ledge. It was like trying to lift a small rhino.

Sheba, in comparison, was light as a feather. She slipped into the room without a sound, and the four of them padded between the beds and out into a corridor.

'Sick people smell funny,' Pyewacket whispered, wrinkling his nose as they left the ward.

'You should try being shut in a small wooden crate with *you* for a few hours,' Inji whispered back. She opened the door at the end of the wing, and they went through, into a stairwell. Tiptoeing as quietly as they could, they headed up the stairs.

'Fourth door down,' Sheba whispered, as they stepped out on to the next floor. This corridor had rich carpets, and brass plaques on the walls with the doctors' names etched on them. It was dark and silent, except for the sliver of light blinking at the bottom of Sir William Jenner's office door.

Inji hardly dared breathe as they moved to stand outside the doorway. She tensed her hands, readying her claws for scratching. Sheba had her pistol drawn and Pyewacket had fished the last remaining stink bomb from his pocket. He held it in the air and gave her a cheeky wink.

They watched Sheba's fingers as she raised them: one, two . . . *three.*

She grabbed the handle and shoved, then they all dashed into the room, teeth bared, weapons raised.

*

Jenner's office was as fancy as you might expect. Framed paintings and expensive rugs. Walnut and brass gleaming everywhere.

It was lit by a single bullseye lamp, which sat on the mahogany desk. Behind it was an open safe, papers hanging out, ransacked. And in the centre of the room was Glyph. He sat cross-legged on the floor, his face pale, eyes wide with terror. On the carpet in front of him were six of his cards, face up, showing a series of numbers. The combination code his captor must have just used to open the safe.

'Ye're a clever bunch of nosy parkers, aren't yeh?'

Inji tore her eyes from the welcome sight of Glyph to the figure standing by Jenner's desk. A familiar face, dressed all in black, with her wild eyes and thick mane of feathered hair.

'Macha,' Inji said. 'So *you're* Gwydion!'

The woman cocked her head like a bird and then

laughed. It sounded like the cawing of a crow, just before it swooped in to peck out your eyes.

'Me? One of those daft toffs with the silly masks? Don't be stupid. Gwydion's over *there.*'

The office door swung shut with a bang. There, appearing from behind it, was the last of the hunters. Inji recognised the bulky leather coat, the smoked-glass goggles and the face mask with its grey fur and wolf's ears.

'Don't move,' he said. In his right hand was a pistol, quicker and more deadly than any crossbow. Under his other arm was a folder of thick manila card, bulging with papers. *The thing he stole from the safe*, Inji thought. *The prize he kidnapped Glyph and Sil for.*

She wondered what information it could hold that was so important. All she could see from here were some letters on the front: F.A.A.C.E.

A code? An acronym? But what did it stand for?

'Put the gun down,' said Sheba. Her voice sounded tired, sad. Not the growling anger Inji would have expected. 'If you come quietly, no one needs to get hurt.'

'If *you* hadn't stuck your noses in, nobody

would have been hurt,' said Gwydion. His voice was muffled by the mask, but Inji was sure she still recognised it. She was about to call Lord Garrow out, when Pyewacket interrupted.

'Your mates have all been nobbled,' he said. 'They're on their way to a new life . . . as transported convicts. How d'you like those apples?'

Gwydion shrugged. 'I couldn't care less about those oafs. They were just the means to an end. Spiteful, cruel monsters, taking joy from hurting other living things. Like schoolboys pulling the legs off spiders. Good riddance to them.'

'But . . . but . . .' Inji couldn't believe what she was hearing. They'd captured the rest of his club. He'd been beaten. She'd expected rage or sorrow. At least some kind of ranting. Why wasn't anyone acting the way they were supposed to?

'Surprised?' Gwydion waved the folder at them. 'They were just idiots I used to get *this*. And now you have all become witnesses. If only you'd stayed away.'

'Please,' said Sheba. 'Put the gun down and we can talk.'

'No talking.' Gwydion tucked the folder under

his gun arm and drew a round object from his jacket pocket. A ball? A bomb? 'Macha,' he said. 'Dispose of them.'

As the bird-woman raised her talons, glinting in the lamplight, Gwydion threw the ball on to the floor. It exploded in a cloud of pale grey smoke that gushed out to fill the room. It rushed into Inji's eyes, making them blink and water. She heard the office door open, then slam. She sensed the shape of Macha moving towards them, just a blur through the smoke.

'Get back!' Inji heard Sheba shout. There was a *swish* as something sliced through the air, drawing whirling patterns in the smoke. Sheba screamed.

'Sheba!' Inji looked around for her, but could see only misty outlines. Then one of the windows *thunked* open and fresh air flooded into the room. The smoke suddenly thinned.

Now Inji could see.

Pyewacket was by the window, coughing and spluttering. Macha was standing near Sheba, one hand raised, talons ready to strike. The other was caught in the strap of Sheba's satchel, spatters of blood all over it.

'No!' Inji shouted, seeing Macha's claws begin

to fall. She realised, with sudden, certain horror, that they were about to plunge into Sheba's neck, and that she was too far away to stop it. She reached out a hand, willing her body to somehow cross the distance in time . . .

Macha suddenly jerked backwards, struck in the waist by something fast and very, very heavy. Her claws came down on to an armour-cased shell, made of thick bone and leathery skin.

Sil. An angry, charging Sil.

The blow had knocked Macha back into the desk and pinned her there. But her taloned hands were still free. She scrabbled with them, trying to find a gap in Sil's armour, reaching around to get at the softer skin of his face, his eyes.

A small, round object flew across the room and hit Macha in the forehead. There was a tinkle of breaking glass, and another cloud of thick smoke blossomed. This time it was purple, and stank like an overflowing privy. Pyewacket had unleashed his last stink bomb.

'Eat that!' he shouted. Everybody in the room clamped their hands over their noses as Macha collapsed on the floor, retching and choking.

But the window was still open and the smell wouldn't last.

'Sil!' Inji called to her brother. 'Sit on her! Pin her to the ground!'

Sil nodded. He jumped into the air and came down on the coughing Macha's back, crushing her to the floor. Then he made himself comfortable, stretching out on her as if she were a feathery, furious blanket.

'Get … off … me!' she croaked. Her hands flapped, trying to bend behind her and get at Sil, but she was completely pinned.

'Here.' Sheba gave Pyewacket her pistol. 'Hold this on her. Make sure she doesn't escape.'

'Where are you going?' Pyewacket asked, taking the gun and checking it was cocked.

'After Gwydion,' said Sheba. 'Coming, Inji?'

'But your arm …' Inji said. There were slash marks on her jacket, and specks of blood among the torn material.

'Just a scratch,' said Sheba. 'The satchel blocked most of it. Come on. He's getting away.'

Inji looked more closely at Sheba's face. Her eyes were gleaming orange and … were those hairs appearing on her brow, on her cheeks?

'Right behind you,' she said. And in her head, the cat flexed its hunting claws.

Chapter Fifteen

Which features London Bridge and quite a bit of falling down.

There was no time for stealth any more. They clattered down the staircase and along the ground-floor corridor. A few yards away, broken glass glinted in a pool of gaslight. Gwydion had smashed a window to escape.

It was only when they were clambering through that Inji noticed they had a follower. A skinny one with a velvet jacket and a huge mop of frizzy curls.

'Glyph, what are you doing? It isn't safe! You should stay here with Sil and Pyewacket.'

Glyph looked at her and shook his head once. His jaw was set and a deep frown line creased his brow. *I'm not going anywhere.*

Inji had no time to argue. She grabbed him under the arms and passed him through the window to Sheba.

'When we catch Gwydion, you need to stay back,' Inji told him. 'Let me and Sheba take care of the fighting.'

She thought she heard a whispered grunt, but then they were off again, running across the courtyard to the open gate, Glyph tailing them like a shadow.

'Oi!' A shout echoed between the sleeping buildings. 'Stop right there!'

Inji looked over her shoulder to see a night-watchman. He was running out of the hospital entrance, holding a lantern.

'We're after a burglar!' Sheba yelled back at him, without breaking her stride. 'We've caught one already! My friends have her pinned down in Sir William's office! Fetch the police!'

The nightwatchman skidded to a halt, looking to the west wing with its broken window and back at the fleeing figures. Clearly, he couldn't decide who to chase, but by the time he'd managed to move his feet, Inji and the others were gone.

They ran out of the gate, turning left down St Thomas Street. The hansom cab still stood there, horseless. Gwydion would have had to flee on foot.

'Where is he?' Inji asked. 'I can't see him anywhere!'

'I have his scent,' said Sheba. 'This way.'

They started running towards London Bridge. Inji could hear the sound of horns and chugging engines. The boats on the river were beginning to wake up and begin the day's work.

'Sheba. His scent . . .' Inji tried to run and speak at the same time. 'You *must* know it's Lord Garrow now?'

Sheba didn't reply.

They turned right on to Borough High Street. Just ahead, running past St Saviour's Church, they saw a figure. A man in hunting leathers, two pointed ears jutting from his head.

'There he is,' Sheba growled. She took hold of her peaked cap and flung it aside, then pulled out the metal combs that had been holding her hair in place. As her curls tumbled down her back, Inji noticed the sharp edges of the combs glinting. They were actually some kind of knives.

The figure looked over his shoulder and spotted them. He began to pick up his pace, running for the bridge. Inji and Sheba sped up too, sprinting along the cracked pavement with the very last of their energy, Glyph scampering behind.

As they reached the bridge, they had closed the gap on Gwydion to just ten yards. There were lamp posts dotted along either side of the road, and Inji could see the rims of his goggles gleaming. The folder was still under his arm, the pistol in his hand. The bridge itself was deserted, although it wouldn't be for long. Soon dawn would come, and with it a tidal wave of people, bustling their way to work.

'A bit closer ...' Sheba panted, putting on a last burst of speed. When she was within range, she wound back her arm and let one of the silver knife-combs fly. It whistled through the air and struck Gwydion in the leg.

He cried out and stumbled against the stone balustrade of the bridge. Then he whirled, gun in hand, and fired.

BANG!

Inji felt a sledgehammer blow hit her shoulder, knocking her backwards through the air and slamming her on to the cobbles. Her head spun, her vision wobbled. What had just happened?

She tried to sit up, but her shoulder was burning. She put a hand there and it came away wet. Had she fallen in a puddle? Why was it sticky?

Looking around, she tried to make sense of her surroundings, why she was lying on the floor . . . and then Glyph was with her, raising her head, helping her sit up.

I've been shot. Gwydion shot me. Her head began to clear, the pain in her shoulder suddenly swelled. She clutched it, feeling the bones grind, and let out a moan.

Glyph tugged her other arm. He was pointing along the bridge.

Shaking her head to clear it, Inji saw Gwydion limping towards them, gun in hand. He was raising it at Sheba, taking aim . . .

But Sheba was moving, dropping down to one knee. She flicked her wrist, and the second comb arced through the air, thudding into his arm. Gwydion's pistol tumbled out of his grip, clattering to the road.

'Damn you!' he roared. With the comb still jutting from his wrist, he moved to pick the gun up again.

'Lucas!' Sheba shouted. 'Lucas, no!'

That made him pause. He looked at Sheba, and then reached up to pull his mask and goggles away. Underneath was the smooth, handsome face of Lucas Garrow, now twisted into an angry snarl, his perfect blond hair tousled and spiked with sweat.

'What gave it away?' he said. 'It was Macha, wasn't it? I should have made her wear a mask too.'

'It was your scent,' said Sheba, pointing at her wolfish nose. 'Although I had guessed before then. When you took Glyph and Sil. It could have been your father – Macha clearly told him everything – and you two were the only ones who knew they would be in our house, all alone. But the plan to go after the other hunters was *yours*. You made it up to get us out of the way. And the stink bombs . . . they were meant to fade so I couldn't follow the trail, weren't they?'

Garrow chuckled. 'I made up that part on the spot. They *were* really meant as a gift for Pyewacket, to get me in your good graces, I admit. But when I saw you had the child I'd been seeking . . .

'After Macha suggested luring the hunters out, I instantly realised it was the perfect way to get to him without you being around. Yes, I knew the bombs would lose their potency in the air, scuppering your plan. I didn't want you harmed, Sheba. I thought you'd spend the night running aimlessly around London. Although I seem to have underestimated your powers as a tracker. The Yard's own bloodhounds couldn't have done better.'

'But Inji and Pyewacket!' Sheba cried. 'Your friends would have killed them!'

'They would.' Garrow shrugged. 'But their lives don't really mean anything. Not compared to what I am trying to achieve for the rest of our kind.'

'And what's that? What is in that file that's so precious to you?'

Garrow took the folder from under his arm and waved it in the air. 'This? Can't you guess? Come on, Sheba. Use that detective's mind of yours.'

'It's medical records,' said Sheba. 'For someone important. A person who has a secret to hide.'

'Wait a minute,' Inji said. Her voice croaked and her legs shook, but she managed to struggle to her feet. 'You said "our kind". What are you talking about? How are you anything like Sheba? And Glyph . . . you were *seeking* him? Why?'

Garrow's eyes narrowed as he sneered at Inji. 'To open Jenner's safe, of course. I knew what was in there. He'd told me one night at the gentlemen's club, when I'd got him drunk on whisky. But I needed the file itself . . . for *proof*.

'Because *I'm* like you. And especially like Sheba.' He turned to her, half smiling. 'That curse which plagues you – the wolf – it's the same with me. As it was with your mother. Why do you think my father hates you so? Why do you think he wants to keep us apart? The Gift runs in our family. Although Father thinks it's a curse. Perhaps because he'll never know the freedom, the *power* of having such wildness in his blood.'

'I . . . I don't believe you.' Sheba took a step back from Garrow, staggered and almost fell.

'I can prove it.' Garrow began a low, growling sound in his throat. As Inji watched, his nose began to jut forward, snoutlike, and his teeth stretched out into fangs. Then he relaxed, and his face shifted back to its perfect, chiselled self.

'You see?' he said. 'We *are* the same. Packmates,

if you will. And we're not the only ones. Besides your . . . *friends* . . . there are many like us, but nobles and highborns. And fierce warriors like Macha. Imagine if we all came together? We could rule this country like wolves among sheep. And then we'd never have to hide or be ashamed again!'

'But how can the file help you do that?' Inji staggered closer to Sheba, still clutching her shoulder. She could feel hot blood running over her fingers.

'Like I said: we're not the only ones. The person in this file is *so* famous, *so* important . . . when the truth comes out about him, we will be able to step out of the shadows. If someone like this can be . . . *gifted*, as you call it . . . then we will all be accepted. Sheba, you should be helping me, not fighting me!'

'But Lucas, you've gone too far! The Hunters' Club . . . they *killed* people! People just like us! Why were you with them?'

'To find *him*, of course!' Garrow pointed a finger at Glyph. 'It was the easiest way to get into the safe. It was supposed to be quick and clean. No criminals involved, no explosives . . . but now you've turned it into a disaster!'

'How did you even know about Glyph?' Inji asked. 'How did you know what he can do?'

At this, Garrow gave a bitter laugh. 'Because he's my *son.*'

Sheba and Inji both gasped.

'Shocked, ladies?' Garrow laughed again. 'It's not a fact I'm proud of. His mother was a servant in my house. My father brought her back from the West Indies. The stupid woman actually thought I loved her . . . that I would give up my fortune and marry her. Of course, when the child was born, my father cast her out. She ended up living on the streets, as you might expect. I had people keep an eye on her, just in case she tried to blackmail me. That's how I knew the boy had a talent.

'And when I found out where Jenner's file was locked away, I knew I had the perfect safe-breaker at my fingertips. Except then I couldn't find him. His mother had died. He had vanished into thin air . . .

'But I know you common . . . *freaks* . . . always end up in penny gaffs and sideshows. I started trying to track him down, going to those vile dens of savages and commoners every night . . . I couldn't stand it.

'Until, one afternoon, I heard Beecher and

Roebuck boasting at the club. About how they'd found the ultimate prey to hunt: paupers and mudlarks off the streets. It didn't take long to convince them to change their victims to sideshow acts. Especially when I promised to use one of my father's factories to build them new toys. And that toady Fleetwood was only too keen to search through all the slums and back alleys for us. I knew he would stumble across the boy eventually. Which he did: in the grip of a seedy common criminal called Stinker – or something equally stupid – along with your catgirl and her brother.

'But the fool lost him again. He spun us a tale about a mob of fifty ruffians stealing his cart. Too embarrassed to admit he was bested by two youngsters half his size. Although if he had mentioned it was a wolf and an imp who threw poo-balls, I would have known instantly it was you.

'Not that it mattered, in the end. Because I discovered him in *your very house*. Right under my nose. It must have been fate.'

He broke off as Sheba choked back a sob. She was shaking her head slowly, a look of absolute horror on her face. Inji found she was almost crying too. *Poor Glyph . . .*

'Lucas,' Sheba said. 'I *trusted* you. I thought you were my friend, my protector. I thought we had so much in common. But all the while you were hiding your true self: a monster. A heartless fiend. How can someone be so cruel, so callous?'

'Don't be stupid, Sheba.' Garrow took a step towards her. 'I understand it's a shock to hear that I already have a child. I admit it was poor judgement, but I was younger then. Immature. And the woman didn't mean anything to me. She was just a servant. A nobody. We *do* have so much in common. And not just our shared passion for inventing . . . we're both marked by the wolf! We're perfect for each other . . .'

'You're not,' said Inji, through gritted teeth. 'She's lovely and you're *evil*.'

Garrow ignored her. 'Come, Sheba. It's not too late. Let me take care of the witnesses, and then we can work together. Just think of the possibilities with your intelligence and mine! And we could marry, have children. They would be wolves too. I would share everything with you, Sheba. You'd never want for anything again.'

Sheba half choked, half laughed and stepped back from Garrow, shaking her head violently. She looked as though she might be sick at the very thought of what he had suggested.

'Sheba!' His eyes flared ice blue and he moved to grab her with his free hand. 'Come with me *now*!'

Inji moved without thinking. As Garrow reached out for Sheba, she swiped at his arm, her claws stretched as long and sharp as she could tweak them. They raked through his leather jacket, biting into the flesh beneath.

He roared, then brought his foot up to kick her. Inji felt all the air burst from her lungs, and then she was flying again, smashing to the cobbles for the second time that night. The impact made her shoulder scream with fresh pain and gold sparks blossomed before her eyes.

'Don't touch her!' Sheba snarled. Inji looked up from the floor and saw her friend become a wolf. Her face bristled with fur, her mouth gleamed with fangs. And those blazing eyes . . . she struck Garrow across the face, her claws leaving deep furrows.

He yelled again, this time sounding fiercer, more feral. He changed as well, letting his face fold and shift into that of a hideous wolf-man, as ugly as his human features were beautiful. His snout was warped, his fangs jutting and jagged. The gouges Sheba had given him dripped blood.

'Die, then!' he snarled. He leapt up on to the stone balustrade of the bridge, back hunched, the fingers of his outstretched hand twisting into long, thirsty claws. Looking down on all of them with a cold fury, he prepared to leap and tear them into meat.

And then . . . Glyph.

All through Garrow's story he had stood, silently taking it in, hearing how this man – his *father* – had destroyed his mother's life, had treated him like a trained dog. He had gone so still, so quiet, that Inji had forgotten he was there.

Now she saw him reaching into his jacket, just as Garrow was about to leap.

He brought out his cards, held them in one hand, bending the edges backwards between his long, delicate fingers.

What? was all Inji had time to think, and then Glyph pushed his fingers together, sending the whole deck streaming out into the air in a fountain of pasteboard and ink. They poured upwards, smacking into Garrow's face, making him teeter backwards.

His feet slipped on the balustrade, his arms pinwheeling.

Inch by inch he began to topple over, his balance gone. It must have happened in less than a blink, but to Inji it seemed to stretch out forever, like he was falling through treacle.

'Sheba!' he managed to shout, holding out a clawed paw.

Sheba moved towards him, as if to catch his hand and pull him to safety, but at the last instant she snatched the file from under his arm instead.

Inji saw the look on his face, just before he fell. It was suddenly human again, eyes wide in disbelief and horror.

And then he was gone.

Where he'd been flailing just an instant before, there was now an empty patch of night, wisps of smog curling to fill the gap.

Inji felt her heart beat once, twice ... and then came the sound of a distant splash.

She lay back on the cobbles and looked up at

the London sky, listening for the sounds of Garrow swimming safely to the shore.

But they never came.

Chapter Sixteen

In which the Carnival officially gains three new members.

The walk back to the hospital was silent.

Dawn was breaking and the London sky was starting to lighten. People were heading out on to the streets, bustling about their business. Lamplighters were out with their ladders, snuffing out the gas-powered street lights. Horses and carts were beginning to clop up and down the roads, beginning the build-up of noise that would soon be thrumming through the city like a bad headache.

Inji clutched her shoulder, feeling weaker and dizzier with each step. Sheba's face was also pale, her hair wild about her shoulders, her jacket ripped and torn.

Glyph took Sheba's hand as he walked beside her. *They're family now*, Inji thought, and it made her smile. At least some good had come out of all the fighting and terror.

They were just turning back into St Thomas Street when Inji, from the corner of her eye, saw Sheba open the precious file. She scanned the first page, eyes wide, and then quickly ripped it out, shoving it inside her jacket. Then she flipped the folder closed and put it back under her arm, as if nothing had happened.

When they reached Guy's, they could see the courtyard was now packed with policemen, along with two wagons and a carriage. The windows were full of patients' faces, peering down at the scene below.

'Stop right there,' said an officer in his dark blue uniform and stovepipe hat. He was guarding the entrance to the hospital, blocking anybody who tried to peer through the gate.

'We're the Carnival,' said Sheba, her voice weary. 'We're the ones who stopped the burglary.'

The policeman looked them up and down, frowning. If it wasn't for the folder under Sheba's arm, he probably would have sent them packing as a bunch of tattered street urchins.

'Let them in, officer!' one of the men inside the courtyard called across. The policeman shrugged and moved aside, allowing them to pass.

As they stepped through the gate, Inji spotted Pyewacket and Sil. They were standing with a group of peelers, who were writing down everything Pyewacket said in their notebooks. He looked like he was enjoying himself immensely.

'Inji!' When Sil saw her, he came running over. She managed to put an arm around him, but winced when he squeezed her.

'Sheebs!' Pyewacket called out. 'Are you all right? Did you get him?'

Sheba nodded.

'Well? Was it Lord Garrow? Don't leave us in suspenders!'

'It was Lucas,' said Sheba, her voice little more than a whisper. 'His son.'

Pyewacket's face fell. 'Oh,' he said. 'Oh, Sheba. I'm sorry.'

'And can you tell us Mr Garrow's whereabouts now?' One of the men who had been interviewing

Pyewacket stepped forward. Unlike the uniformed officers, he wore a checked three-piece suit with a brown overcoat and top hat. Beneath the brim were quick, dark eyes and a splendidly bushy moustache.

'Who are you?' Sheba said, her usual manners forgotten. The man pulled a wallet out of his pocket and flipped it open.

'Inspector Abernathy,' he said. 'Of Scotland Yard. Mr Garrow?'

'He's dead,' said Inji. 'He fell in the river.'

'Ah.' Abernathy beckoned two of the uniformed officers over. 'Get a boat out, lads. See if you can fish what's left of young Garrow out, before the eels get to him.'

As the officers strode off, Abernathy's eyes fell on the folder Sheba was still holding. 'I see you have retrieved the stolen property,' he said.

Sheba nodded and handed the folder over. Abernathy opened it and flicked through a few pages, his eyebrows rising just a fraction.

'Very good,' he said. 'I'll see this gets returned. You wouldn't happen to have looked inside it, would you?'

'Of course not,' said Sheba, her face completely

straight. Inji pretended to wince at the pain in her shoulder, just in case she accidentally gave the game away.

'If you don't mind, Inspector,' said Sheba. 'My young friend here needs medical attention. She's been shot.'

'Yes, yes, right away,' said Abernathy. 'You ... *investigators*, as your associate said you were ... have done the hospital – and the city – a great service tonight. I will make sure you're taken care of, don't worry.'

With a gentle hand on Inji's back, Abernathy led them across the courtyard to the hospital's main entrance. As they passed a heavy police wagon with barred windows, Inji saw Macha being shoved inside. Her hands were cuffed and her face was dark as a thunderstorm.

I hope they lock you up and throw away the key, Inji thought. *Cats beat birds after all.*

There was a kindly nurse waiting for them at the hospital door, and then a bed and bandages ... and finally deep, deep, welcome sleep.

*

When Inji woke up, what seemed like days later, she was snug in a feather bed, in a little room with a sloping roof and big windows. Sheba was sitting next to her on a stool, tinkering with some mechanism. Screwdrivers and pencils poked out of her hair bun and there was a smudge of grease on her button nose.

She looked up to see Inji staring at her. 'You're awake!' she said. 'At last.'

'Where am I? The hospital?'

'No,' said Sheba. 'We brought you back to Paradise Street. You slept all the way. That was two days ago.'

'Two days?' Inji couldn't believe it. But then she had been *so* tired. 'Where's Sil?'

'Downstairs with Pyewacket,' said Sheba. 'I believe Pyewacket's trying to make Glyph spell out the winner of next year's Grand National so he can win himself a fortune.'

A shout came from the stairwell, cutting Sheba off.

'What's that? A huntsman?[xii] Is that supposed to be some kind of joke? After I've just been chased through the midnight woods by a bunch of them?

Are you *trying* to give me a heart attack, you little blighter?!'

'So sorry,' said Sheba, wincing.

'As long as Sil's all right,' said Inji. 'Has there been any other news?'

Sheba nodded, her face grim. 'They found Lucas's body in the river,' she said. 'But the other hunters are still missing. It's quite the scandal in the papers. Three noblemen and their friend vanishing from the face of the earth. Of course, no one knows they were really the Hunters' Club.'

'What about Macha?'

'She's being blamed for the burglary,' said Sheba. 'I expect she'll receive a long prison sentence. Maybe worse. They've kept Lucas's involvement quiet, however. The story is that he fell in the river from his yacht. Terrible accident.'

'And the folder?'

'Not even mentioned,' said Sheba. 'And we had best not talk about it, either.'

Inji sat up in bed and looked around the room. It had a dressing table, a bookshelf and a wardrobe. Sunlight danced across the rugs on the floor. 'What is this place?' she said. 'I've never seen it before.'

'This?' Sheba said, smiling. 'It's one of the attic rooms. *Your* room. If you want it?'

'You mean . . . ?' The words stuck in Inji's throat for a moment. 'You mean I can stay? And Sil? And Glyph?'

'Of course,' said Sheba. 'Glyph is my family, after all. Actually . . . you and Sil are my family too.'

'Really?' Inji couldn't bring herself to believe it. When did things like this ever happen to her? 'Do you actually mean it?'

'Inji,' said Sheba. 'This world has so much darkness in it. Sideshow owners, baby farmers, hunters . . . people who put their own pleasure and profit above the lives of everyone else. But there's light here too. And when people like us find each other, help each other . . . then the light is much, much stronger than the dark. After all, what is darkness but a lack of light? That's what I think, anyway. That's what being a part of the Carnival taught me. And what I want to teach you.'

'But . . .' Inji needed to hear it in simple words, in black and white. 'We *can* stay, though? Forever?'

'Forever.'

She took hold of Sheba's hand and held it tight for a long, long while.

*

The next few months passed quietly as the newest Carnival members settled in.

The boys had been given a room next to Sheba's. It took a few weeks, but they finally became used to sleeping in beds, rather than on the floor.

Sil adapted to his new life much more quickly than Inji would have thought. The bacon sandwiches helped, and Sheba got him as many maps as she could find: London, Paris, New York, Hong Kong. He sat for hours, tracing the streets. He even began to draw his own maps in notebooks. Intricate pencil lines of roads and houses, spidering over every inch. It was the happiest he had ever been, Inji thought, which made her happy too.

Glyph had a new set of pasteboard cards, blank ones, which he spent many weeks inking with letters and numbers. Sheba taught him some sign language, but he still preferred to use the cards, much to Pyewacket's delight. He soon had a collection of lockboxes, which Glyph could find the combination for, no matter how many numbers there were. Inji supposed it was a better way to pass the time than trying to cheat at horse races.

Inji started learning to meditate. She found that it did indeed help her control her cat-ness. It even seemed, as she peered in the mirror, that her skin appeared a touch less furry, the stripes more faint. Although her eyes . . . well, they would never change. She found the thought didn't bother her so much any more. Not now she had a family just like her.

And other friends too. A postcard had arrived from Edinburgh: Mama Rat and Gigantus were there with the Scarlequins and had heard the news about Lucas Garrow. They gave their condolences, and promised to return to London before Christmas, now that the city was safe for them once more.

It was the most peaceful, most secure Inji had ever felt. And yet a tiny thorn still niggled at her. One last snaggly thread of doubt about the hunters and their evil club.

Whose folder had Garrow stolen? Who was the important person that was different, like them?

The answer came halfway through December. They were all having breakfast in the parlour when Pyewacket came running in, waving a newspaper.

'He's dead!' Pyewacket cried. 'Prince Albert's gone and died!'

Sheba snatched the paper and read the front page. She looked shocked and pale. Wondering why, Inji peered over her shoulder.

Prince Consort Dies at Windsor Castle, it read. *Doctors diagnose typhoid fever.* Further down, it listed Albert's full and proper name: *Francis Albert Augustus Charles Emmanuel.*

F.A.A.C.E.

Inji clapped her hands over her mouth to hide her gasp, but Sheba had noticed it.

'Inji,' she said. 'Come with me and fetch some more tea.'

The pair walked out of the room, leaving Pyewacket to read the article out to the others. They went down the corridor, but instead of heading into the kitchen, Sheba led Inji down the secret stairs and into the workshop.

'You've worked it out,' she said, when they had reached the bottom.

'Prince Albert,' said Inji. 'That was *his* folder. The one Garrow tried to steal.'

Sheba nodded. She walked to the wall and

pushed one of the shelves. There was a *click* and a hidden hatch opened, revealing an iron safe. Sheba twisted the dial on the front this way and that until it popped open. Inside was the page she had stolen from the folder.

She handed it to Inji. It was covered with doctor's notes in scrawled handwriting, but there was a tintype photograph pasted to the yellow paper. A man, balding, with side whiskers and a moustache. A face she instantly recognised as the Prince Consort. He was standing in his underwear, side on to the camera. And there, hanging down from the base of his back, was a long *tail*.

'He was like *us*,' Inji whispered.

'Indeed,' said Sheba. 'I'm showing you because you figured it out anyway. But this must remain a complete and total secret. You can't even tell Sil. Do you promise?'

Inji nodded. She knew how important the information was. People had already died because of it. 'But why did you take this page?' she asked. 'Wouldn't it be better not to have known?'

'I had to know,' said Sheba. 'I couldn't help myself. I've always been too curious for my own good. But I took the page for insurance. In case anyone threatens us because of what we discovered. We have proof ourselves, and it's a secret that many people will want to stay hidden.'

A sudden, horrid thought occurred to Inji. 'Do you think that's why he's dead? Did someone find out the secret and decide to . . . assassinate him?'

Sheba shook her head. 'I don't know. I wouldn't like to think so, but . . . if Sir William Jenner told Lucas about it, there's a good chance he told someone else. The file being stolen, the prince dying . . . it *does* seem like an odd coincidence.'

Inji passed the page back, her hand shaking slightly.

'Are we in danger?' she asked. 'Will we need to use it?'

'No, I don't think so,' Sheba replied. 'After all, nobody knows we have it. Or that I even looked inside the folder. I'm sure we're safe for now.

'Besides,' she added, giving Inji a smile that showed the sharp points of her canine teeth, 'who would be stupid enough to threaten the Carnival of the Lost?'

Inji smiled back, her own teeth glinting.

Let them try, she thought. *Let them try.*

Epilogue

Throughout London, holly hangs in windows, ivy wreaths on front doors. In the big townhouses of the rich, Christmas trees can be glimpsed in parlours, with buckets of water perched next to them, in case the tiny candle lights burn the house down.

But the usual festive atmosphere is dimmed this year, for today is the funeral of Albert, Prince Consort – the husband of the queen.

Although the ceremony itself is taking place at Windsor, the people of the city are in mourning too. In the hour before midday, they begin to leave their homes and workplaces, making their way towards Westminster Abbey. Dressed in black, they fill the streets in a snaking, inky stream. Voices are muted, heads are bowed. They have come to say farewell to a man they all respected and admired, who brought so much to them in the short time he stood beside the throne.

The sky above is slate grey, with clouds that threaten snow. One or two flakes drift down, wheeling about in the breeze, glaring bright against the sombre darkness everywhere.

A family emerges from a house in Paradise Street. Two adults and three children, all dressed in black, with veils and hats pulled low. One of the children looks a strange shape – bulky and blocky, like a baby rhino has been squeezed into a suit – but they soon merge with the rest of the crowd and blend into the river of blackness.

On a rooftop nearby, a figure stands watching. A woman, wearing a long winter coat with the collar turned up. Like many in the crowd below, she has a veil covering her face, although from beneath hers comes the faint sound of a clockwork engine –*tickticktickticktick*.

She stares after the little group, her breath smoking in the icy air, until long after they have disappeared.

'I hope you enjoy your lives together,' she says, finally. 'Because that will make it all the more painful when I destroy them. When I make you pay for everything you have done.'

And with that, the woman turns and walks back to where an open attic window waits for her. She climbs down into the house below, disappearing from sight.

A few seconds later the first proper snowflakes start to fall, mixing with the smoke and soot. Somewhere in the streets below, a young voice begins to sing a carol. In two days, it will be Christmas, and the city will be painted white, fresh and (for an hour or two, at least) clean.

Like a blank page waiting for a new story to begin.

Notes

i. A rookery was a collection of tumbledown buildings, packed full of very poor people and lots of criminals. Nothing to do with birds at all.

ii. If you didn't have a job or a home, the Victorian version of helping out was to lock you away in a building called a workhouse, where you did pointless, unpleasant jobs all day, like picking rope apart or crushing rocks. Hopefully, you would die of overwork or starvation quite quickly, so you could save the government as much money as possible.

iii. 'Cove' is Victorian slang for a 'chap' or person. They didn't get sold into slavery by a small, sandy beach, nestled among some cliffs.

iv. Tintype was an early method of taking photographs. The image appeared on a thin sheet of metal, which was much quicker to develop and fix than other techniques that used paper.

v. This was a big deal, because most houses had outdoor toilets, and many of those just emptied into pits. A flushing toilet, *indoors*, was the height of luxury.

vi. Fences were people who took stolen goods and sold them on, sharing the profits with the thieves and burglars. Although they didn't do any stealing themselves, the crime was just as serious.

vii. What actually happened, in most cases, was that the baby farmers kept the money and then set about starving the poor babies to death or – in some grisly examples – simply killing them and throwing the bodies in the River Thames.

viii. P. T. Barnum was an American showman (often thought to be the 'Greatest') who had a world-famous sideshow that included acts such as General Tom Thumb and the Fijian Mermaid. He travelled the world with his troupe but, contrary to popular belief, hardly ever did any singing.

ix. Chloroform was an early type of anaesthetic used in some of the first surgical operations.

x. Pure-pickers had the unfortunate job of collecting dogs' mess for tanning leather with.

xi. Butcher's hook = look.

xii. The winner of the 1862 Grand National was, in fact, a horse called The Huntsman. If Pyewacket hadn't been so offended, he could have made himself a millionaire.

Read on for an extract from *The Legend of Podkin One-Ear*. A bard is about to tell the story of a young rabbit who must face the most horrifying enemy rabbitkind has ever known . . .

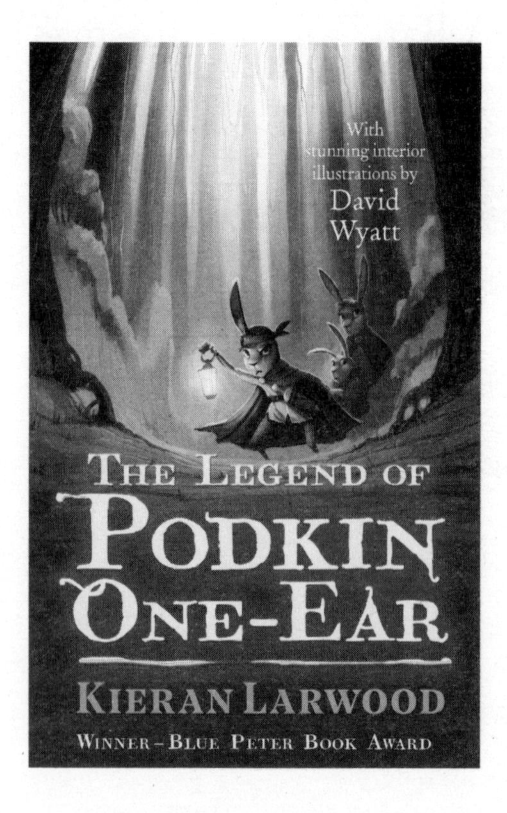

Chapter One

A Bard for Bramblemas

C*runch, crunch. Crunch, crunch.* The sound of heavy footsteps, trudging through knee-deep snow, echoes through the night's silence.

A thick white blanket covers the wide slopes of the band of hills known as the Razorback downs. Moonlight dances over it, glinting here and there in drifts of sparkles, as if someone has sprinkled the whole scene with diamond dust.

It is perfect – untouched except for one spidery line of tracks leading down from the hills towards the frosted woodland beneath.

Crunch, crunch. Crunch, crunch go the footsteps of the track-maker. He is hunched and weary, using a tall staff to help him through the snow. He might have been an old man, if it hadn't been many hundreds of moons since men trod these lands. Move closer and instead you will see he is a rabbit, walking upright in the way men once did, his ears hidden beneath the hood of a heavy leather cloak, fierce eyes peering out at the wintry midnight world.

The thick fur on his face and arms is dyed with blue swirls and patterns, which marks him out as a bard. A travelling, storytelling rabbit. A wanderer with nothing on his back but a set of travel-worn clothes and a head stuffed full of tales and yarns: old, new, broken and mended. Just about every story you ever heard, and many more yet to be told.

Don't worry about him being out in the cold on such a wintry night. His trade will see him welcomed in any warren. That is the tradition and the law throughout all of the Five Realms of Lanica, and woe betide anyone who doesn't keep it.

Crunch, crunch. Crunch, crunch. His breath steams out behind him as he forces his way through the snow. Listen closer and you can hear him mumbling curses with each hard-fought step. Closer still and you can hear the strings of wooden beads around his neck clicking and clacking. The bone trinkets and pouches around his belt knocking and niggling.

He marches with a purpose, as if he has someplace to be and he is already late. But where is there for him to go? There is nothing but snow and trees from here all the way to the horizon. Until, of course, you remember that he's a rabbit. Rabbits live underground, in warrens and burrows: warm and safe, out of the winter ice and frost.

And that is indeed where he is heading. Into the woods and through the trees until he stops before a pair of huge entrance doors, set into the side of a little hill. Behind them is Thornwood Warren, and there had better be a warm welcome for him, or there will be serious trouble.

Boom, boom, boom! He smacks the end of his staff against the oak and waits for an answer.

Back when rabbits were small, twitchy, terrified things, warrens were little more than a collection of holes and tunnels in the ground. Now, in this new age, they are something different altogether: there are entire villages and cities built under the earth, completely out of sight.

The bard knew that behind those wooden doors would be nest-burrows and market-burrows, workshops, temples, libraries, larders, pantries and a dozen kitchens to feed them all. There would be soldiers and healers, servants, cooks, smiths, weavers, tailors, potters and painters. Old rabbits, young rabbits, poor rabbits and noble rabbits. All walks of life hidden away in cosy, torch-lit, underground houses; all arranged around every warren's hub: the longburrow, a great feasting hall with a huge fireplace, rows of tables and nearly always music. Music, noise and merriness – that is what rabbits love. Especially tonight, for this was Bramblemas Eve: the night on which the winter solstice was celebrated with a special feast, and the promise of presents in the morning, left behind by the mysterious Midwinter Rabbit.

And stories of course. Special stories, told by a visiting bard – that is, if he ever got inside the place.